ALAN C. PORTER

THE LOST PATROL

Complete and Unabridged

LINFORD
Leicester

First published in Great Britain in 2005 by
Robert Hale Limited
London

First Linford Edition
published 2006
by arrangement with
Robert Hale Limited
London

British Library CIP Data

Porter, Alan C., *1959* –
   The lost patrol.—Large print ed.—
   Linford western library
   1. Western stories
   2. Large type books
   I. Title
   823.9′14 [F]

   ISBN 1–84617–397–3

Published by
F. A. Thorpe (Publishing)
Anstey, Leicestershire

Set by Words & Graphics Ltd.
Anstey, Leicestershire
Printed and bound in Great Britain by
T. J. International Ltd., Padstow, Cornwall

1

Water sprayed from the metal-rimmed wheels and from beneath the pounding, iron-shod hoofs of the team of six. Hat pulled down as far as possible, Jake sat hunched in a yellow slicker on the driving-seat of the stage as the rain hammered down from a leaden sky.

The trail was rapidly becoming a quagmire. Once or twice the stage had slithered sideways on a fountain of mud and water as it had taken tight bends, but Jake refused to slow down, pushing the team on at an even more reckless speed.

Inside the stage Sheriff Tom Morgan braced himself in one corner as it lurched from side to side.

'Dammit, Jake, slow down!' he bellowed. If Jake heard he paid no attention. In the other corner Deputy Cal Brice threw Tom a look.

'Reckon ol' Jake's in a hurry some, Sheriff, and I wonder why?' He let his gaze drift to the third occupant. 'What do you reckon, Small? Could be he's real anxious to see 'the Butcher of Prospect' behind bars.' He leered at the third occupant of the stage. Ethan Small was a big, powerfully built individual in his mid-forties, clad in dirty range clothes. Manacles encircled his wrists and ankles, the thick bands of metal and stout chains looking frail against his big frame.

The two sets of manacles were joined together by a third length of thick chain that did not allow the man to lift his arms above waist level. These measures were felt necessary as Small had already escaped once and this time they were taking no chances. He was being taken back to Prospect to stand trial for a vicious double murder. As if the chains were not enough, his boots had been removed as an added precaution against trying to escape on foot.

Ethan Small sat in the centre of the

seat opposite the sheriff and his deputy. His bare feet were planted firmly on the floor, his shoulders pressed back into the seat as he rode the lurching stage, chain links rattling, head tilted down.

'Reckon he's plumb anxious to get to a hanging,' Cal Brice spoke up. He smiled unpleasantly and settled a glance on Ethan Small. 'You're gonna hang, Small, for sure. The trial's just a formality.' He gave a chuckle, but the chuckle faded as the prisoner failed to respond.

'I'm talking to you, killer. What do you say?' Still no response. 'Dammit, Small, d'yer hear me?' This time he raised a foot and slammed it against Ethan's left knee.

Tom glared across at Brice.

'Quit it, Cal,' he said sharply.

'Jus' having a conversation wi' the Butcher here,' Cal replied. 'Why'd you kill 'em, Small? What had they ever done to you to make you take a knife to 'em an' then try an' burn them so no one would ever find out?'

Ethan Small raised his head and looked squarely at the taunting deputy.

'I didn't kill anybody,' he said softly.

'Sure you didn't, that's why theys'a gonna hang you,' Brice jeered. 'Had it my way I'd put a bullet in your useless hide now an' save the town some money.'

'Cal, ain't you hearing what I'm saying? Leave the man alone,' Tom snapped harshly, fixing his deputy with a hard, unremitting stare. 'Got me 'nough o' Jake's driving wi'out you jawing on. D'yer get what I'm saying?'

Cal sniffed and wriggled uncomfortably, pressing himself into the corner and bracing one foot on the opposite seat as the stage lurched and rocked wildly.

'Jus' making conversation,' the deputy mumbled. By now the prisoner had lost interest and had sunk his head on to his chest, letting it roll with every lurch and shudder of the wildly driven stage.

Tom could understand Cal Brice's treatment of the prisoner. He had been on duty when Small had escaped and that rankled with the deputy. Had it not been for the keen eyes of a lawman in the next county, Small might have got away. As it was he spent ten days on the run before capture.

Tom stared at the prisoner. He had known Ethan Small as a quiet, amiable man. Damnit, they had been friends! He, Tom Morgan, had been seeing Small's daughter, Emma. He had never known Ethan raise his voice in anger or show signs of temper even when provoked, yet here he was accused of the murder of Jed Blake and his wife.

Tom prided himself on being a shrewd judge of character and he would have sworn on a stack of bibles that it was not in Small's nature to hurt anyone, yet the evidence was damning. Small's knife was found jutting from the stabbed and slashed body of Jed Blake. A bloodstained shirt belonging to Small was discovered in a barn on Small's property, but most damning of all was the name Jed Blake had managed to scrawl with his own blood on the door of the woodshed: SMALL before he had died, with his house in flames and his wife within.

Even with the evidence, Tom still found it hard to accept, or maybe because of it. It was all so neat and tidy. The knife, shirt, name. Too neat and tidy, but it wasn't up to him to judge. It was his job to bring the man in and let the due process of the law take its course.

The stage lurched wildly as it took a bend at speed. Jake squinted through the driving rain. Too late he saw that the trail ahead was washed out.

He hauled back on the reins and threw the brake-lever, but the leather pads on the wooden brake-blocks failed to have any effect on the mud-slicked wheels. With a yell of terror Jake gave up trying to control the stage. He jumped from the left side as the stage canted steeply to the right sending the unprepared occupants sliding together. Tom Morgan collided with Cal Brice, pinning the man in the corner.

As the stage began to tip, Ethan Small managed to swing his manacled feet on to the seat and brace them against the side of the stage just below the opposite side window.

The angle of the stage steepened on the slippery slope and it slammed down on its right side, the wooden yoke splintering, leather traces snapping, freeing the six-horse team to gallop off into the driving rain.

The stage flipped on to its roof, rolling down the slope towards the river below. A day ago the river had been a gently bubbling stream, now it was a swollen, raging torrent filled with uprooted trees and brush.

Yells and curses came from the stage as the three inside were tumbled and thrown together in the bruising, bone-breaking roll. Two of the wheels shattered on the axle, leaving just a few spokes jutting out while a third broke loose, rolling and bouncing down the slope ahead of the stage.

As it neared the river the front section of the stage hit a tree, tearing the driver's box and a section of panel above the seat away. The stage slewed around, cartwheeled and slid into the swollen river right into the path of a floating tree. Dazed, head singing, Ethan was barely aware of the splintering crash and judder as the side nearest him exploded inwards. Shattered branches like the skeletal fingers of a giant hand were thrust into the stage.

More out of instinct than awareness he threw himself flat on the seat. He heard a cry as water flooded in. The stage turned sideways across the river as a second tree, this one reduced to a log, smashed through the panelling of the other door and drove itself along the narrow aisle between the seats before coming to a halt, skewering the stage like a carcass on a spit.

Muddy water surged in, reaching to seat-level. The stage came to an uneasy halt as one of the trees snagged.

Ethan managed to push himself into

a sitting position. Directly across from him the sheriff sat stiff and upright, held in position by a stout branch that had passed through his right shoulder, pinning him to the back of the seat. Next to him the deputy was dead, his head crushed between the splintered end of the trunk of the same tree and back of the seat. Blood stained the water about the luckless man. The stage creaked and groaned as the water beat with foaming fists at its battered, wooden body.

Sickened at the sight of the dead deputy, Ethan knew that it would only be a matter of minutes before what remained of the stage broke apart and he and Tom Morgan would join Brice. He mentally cursed the chains that held and restricted him. He looked across at Tom Morgan.

'The keys, Tom,' he said urgently lifting his hands as high as he could and pushing them towards the pinioned man. In answer Tom Morgan drew his gun and levelled it at Ethan, thumbing back the hammer.

'Not so fast, Ethan,' he said thickly, pain creasing his face.

Ethan eyed him in surprise.

'What in damnation d'yer think you're gonna do wi' that? Dammit, Tom, stop playing sheriff an' think about staying alive. I can get us out, but not wi' these on.'

The stage lurched, slid a few feet and juddered to a halt. A gasp of pain broke from Tom's lips as the branch pinning him was wrenched in the wound. The gun slid from his grasp as he used both hands to grip the branch. He eyed Ethan.

'Guess I can't stop you,' he grated and released one hand to dig the key from his vest pocket.

Ethan took it with numb fingers. The water that half-filled the stricken stage was ice-cold and precious minutes were lost as he struggled to undo the heavy padlock that secured the length of chain between leg-irons and wrist manacles.

The manacles themselves had been

secured into place by means of hot rivets burred over with a blacksmith's hammer. They would have to be struck off, but such details would have to wait. Gingerly he climbed to his feet and edged closer to the tree that held Tom in its grasp. The branch was an inch or more thick.

'You gotta knife?'

'On my belt,' Tom returned dully.

Ethan found a thick-bladed Bowie knife sheathed at Tom's waist and with quick hands began to slice slivers from where the branch joined the trunk, whittling away, reducing the thickness of the branch until he was able to sever it from the trunk.

Tom's face was white. Every little movement must have sent waves of agony through his shoulder, but apart from the occasional grunt he made no complaint. He looked up at Ethan.

'Why are you doing this, Ethan? Saving me ain't gonna help you none.'

'Like I said, Tom, I didn't kill the Blakes. They were my friends, you know that. The first I knew they were dead was when you came knocking at my door.'

'It was your knife in Jed Blake's back. Your shirt found covered in blood . . . '

'An' my name written in blood. Yeah, I know the evidence agin me, but it wasn't me,' Ethan interupted. 'That's why I broke jail. I was looking to prove my innocence. Trouble is it made me look more guilty.'

The stage lurched and stressed panels groaned. Ethan eyed the two feet of branch that protruded from Tom's shoulder. There was no way he was going to get him out of the stage with that in place.

'It's gonna have to come out, Tom,' he said quietly.

Tom nodded and ran a tongue over his lips.

'Do it!' He barked harshly and closed his eyes as Ethan's big hands closed around the branch.

In one swift move he yanked the length of branch from Tom's shoulder.

This time Tom cried out, unable to help himself as a pulse of agonizing pain ripped through his shoulder. He clapped a hand protectively to it, face screwed into a mask of pain.

'Let me take a look,' Ethan said. He pulled the other's hand aside before using the knife to cut the shirt away after pulling Tom's coat open. Blood pulsed from the wound. 'I've seen worse,' Ethan opined. He pulled the bandanna from Tom's neck, bunched it and pushed it into the other's trembling hand. 'Keep that pressed over it while I get you outta here.'

Half-carrying, half-dragging the injured man Ethan got him to the door then lowered himself into the river. Close to the bank the water was no more than waist-high, but its fast flow threatened to pull his manacled feet out from under him.

Hampered by the log jammed in the doorway and weakened by loss of blood and shock Tom fell into Ethan's waiting arms. Holding the man as if he weighed no more than a baby Ethan shuffled to the bank. It was not a moment too soon for as they gained the safety of the bank, the stage, with a splintering crack, split in half. Both halves were whisked away on the foaming torrent.

Ethan carried the semi-conscious man a few yards to the cover of a stand of trees. He set him down against the bole of one and dropped down beside him breathing heavily. Both men were soaked through. Ethan's clothes were pasted to his body, hair plastered to his scalp by the rain.

'So what happens now?' It was Tom who spoke. Some colour had returned to his cheeks as a numbness settled through his injured shoulder, taking away the pain.

'Gotta get you to a doctor. Mebbe I can catch us some o' them horses.' Ethan didn't sound to confident.

Tom looked at his saviour in surprise.

'Case you're forgettin', you got irons on your legs an' wrists an' no boots. The only thing you'll be catching is a bullet, if'n anyone sees you.'

'You'll never make it on your own,' Ethan returned bluntly.

'When the stage don't turn up they'll come a-looking.' Tom nodded at his own words and lapsed into silence. Then, 'Why would anyone want to kill the Blakes an' set you up as the murderer?' He broke the silence, eyeing Ethan speculatively.

Ethan shrugged. 'For half a million in Confederate gold, mebbe.'

A tired smile stretched Morgan's bearded lips.

'The lost patrol.' He shook his head sadly. 'No one believes that story any more. Sure, fifteen years ago a confederate patrol carrying the gold passed through Prospect heading for the mountains and were never seen again. That's true enough. Some believe the patrol came to grief in the mountains an' the gold's up there somewhere waiting to be found. They've spent the last fifteen years looking for it. Me, I favour a more down-to-earth idea. The

15

men in the patrol took it for themselves.'

'Mebbe,' Ethan agreed, 'but fifteen years ago Jed Blake was a Confederate captain. He was the one who sent the gold. The men in the patrol were diehard Confederates, hand-picked by Blake himself for their loyalty to the Confederacy; one was his brother. They wouldn't have stolen the gold. It was because of his brother that it became a matter of family honour. He spent five years searching the Guadalopes, but never found a trace o' the patrol. In the end he an' his wife moved to Prospect, but he never gave up looking.'

'I never knew.'

'That was the way Jed wanted it, but someone found out. Guess he was poking about an' gotta little too close for someone's comfort.'

Tom's forehead furrowed.

'What exactly are you saying here, Ethan?'

'I'm not saying anything. It was Jed who did all the saying. He was of the opinion that the gold never left Prospect that night. The patrol was murdered, their bodies hid an' the gold took. Figure he was getting close to finding out who, but tipped his hand in the wrong corner an' got himsel' an' his wife killed for his trouble.'

'That's sure one hell o' a statement,' Tom pointed out.

Ethan shrugged. 'I know I never killed Jed an' his wife.'

Tom eyed the other.

'Dammit, Ethan you got me all but convinced. Trouble is you've got the most powerful men in Prospect calling for your blood.'

Ethan smiled grimly.

'Sure makes a body wonder why,' he pointed out softly.

Tom's mouth 'O'd in surprise, then his face dissolved in a mask of agony as a wave of pain flared through his injured shoulder.

'Damnation!' he groaned. He gripped his shoulder as a shudder ripped through his body.

17

Ethan clambered awkwardly to his feet, chains rattling, concern on his face.

'We gotta get you to a doctor.'

As he loomed over the injured man a gun roared. Ethan straightened, arching his shouders as a bullet slammed into his back and exited messily through his chest.

'I got the murdering scum,' Jake, the stage driver, cried out as he slithered down the slope.

Tom could only watch in shocked despair as Ethan sank to his knees clutching his chest before toppling face down into the mud.

'You damn gun-happy fool!' Tom shouted. His own injuries temporarily forgotten he crawled on his knees to Ethan's side and turned the man over.

Ethan's eyes flickered open, the grey pallor of death suffusing the skin of his muddy face. Blood seeped from his lips. He focused his eyes on Tom's face.

'Emma.' It was the first time he had mentioned his own daughter's name.

He clawed weakly at Tom's arm. 'Look out for her, Tom,' he implored, his whispered words almost lost in the rush of the swirling river and patter of rain. He smiled briefly then his head lolled to one side and his grip fell away.

Tom gently lowered the dead man's head to the ground and sat back on his calves.

'Thought he was gonna kill you,' Jake said defensively.

Tom eyed the man as a surge of intense pain tore through him and then his world dissolved into silent darkness as unconsciousness claimed him.

2

It took almost two weeks before Tom had recovered enough to step out on to the streets of Prospect. Arm in a sling, it was good to feel the sun on his face again. Another day cooped up in that hotel room would have sent him mad.

'You ain't ready to be up an' about yet,' Doc Maddison had protested, but his protest had fallen on deaf ears. Now as Tom steadied himself at the hitching-rail he felt there was some wisdom in Doc's words, but was not about to admit it.

His legs felt as weak as a new born colt's but that was only to be expected after two weeks in bed. Taking deep breaths of the warm, dusty air he walked along the sidewalk towards his office. He was anxious to get back to work. Word had reached him that with his deputy dead and he himself laid up,

Hoyt Nokes had been made acting sheriff and that was a bitter pill to swallow.

Nokes was a bully and a coward and on two occasions Tom had thrown him into jail for being drunk and disorderly. It didn't make sense. Why would the town council appoint such a man?

People called out to him as he passed. He acknowledged their greetings with the wave of a hand.

'Good to see you back on your feet, Tom,' Seth Haggerman called out from the front of his general store.

'Good to be back on 'em,' Tom replied.

The sheriff's office lay opposite the bank and was flanked on one side by a draper's shop and on the other, separated by a narrow alley, Mary's hash-house. By the time he reached the office he was sweating profusely and his legs were protesting more heartily than the good doctor.

Hoyt Nokes raised his head as the door opened and surprise flared briefly in his small, deep-set eyes as Tom entered. Nokes lounged in a tilted-back chair, feet crossed and resting on the old battered desk, hands clasped across his ample stomach. The small office reeked of stale cigar smoke.

'Never knowed you wus comin' in today,' he stated flatly as Tom approached the desk.

'Didn't know it mysel' until I woke up this morning,' Tom replied crisply. 'Now how 'bout you getting your feet offa my desk an' your butt outta my chair?'

Nokes smiled nastily.

'Now is that the way to speak to your new sheriff, boy?' He arched an eyebrow.

Tom stepped closer to the desk, anger flaring in his eyes.

'You ain't my sheriff, Nokes. Now move yourself or I'll throw you in jail for obstucting the law.'

'Cain't do that, Morgan. Mayor Tully made me sheriff. Said you weren't coming back . . . ever.' He jerked a thumb at the badge on his chest. 'This here's a sheriff's star. You figure you can take it off me an' pin it on your own vest?'

Tom clenched his good fist at his side in impotent fury as Nokes taunted him. Any retort he might have made was forestalled by the door opening behind him. He turned and found himself facing a tall, powerfully built man in grubby range clothes.

'Reckon you know my deputy, Mitch Colson,' Nokes sang out, grinning broadly at Tom's back.

Tom gaped at Colson, not believing what he was seeing or hearing. It was bad enough finding Nokes in his chair, but to be facing Colson, the man wearing a shiny deputy's star on his chest, turned the situation into a nightmare.

Colson had spent more time in jail than Nokes. Finding both of them parading about as lawmen was beyond his comprehension.

Colson, a cigar-butt clenched between

his stubble-ringed lips, smiled coldly at Tom. Strands of lank, black hair spilled from the brim of his hat, curling well below his ears.

'Well if'n it ain't our one-time sheriff. Heard tell you had retired.'

'Figure you've been listening to the wrong people,' Tom snapped back.

Colson studied him from half-closed eyes.

'A one-armed sheriff ain't much use to anyone,' he stated in his slow, measured drawl. 'Hell! A one-armed sheriff is about as useful as a three-legged horse. What d'you reckon, Hoyt?'

'I reckon you said the truth o' it there, Mitch. Now why don' you get outta my office, Morgan, afore I throw you in jail for a breach o' the peace an' imitating a law officer.' Nokes chuckled at his joke and Colson joined it.

'That sure was a good one, Hoyt.'

'We'll see what Mayor Tully has to say 'bout this,' Tom said, tight-lipped.

'You do that, boy.' Nokes nodded his

head and broke into a laugh. 'Three-legged hoss. I like that, I surely do.'

Tom said nothing else and after glaring at both men stamped out of the office. His rage and anger temporarily numbed his own aches and pains as he marched quickly, stiff-backed, in the direction of the mayor's office, ignoring voices that called out greetings to him.

The sound of raised, but muffled voices beyond the door caused Mayor Tully to lift his grey-maned head from the document he was studying. A few seconds later the door burst open and Tom entered the plush office with it's dark, wood-panelled walls and claret-coloured carpeting. Behind him followed a thin stick of a man in a city suit, dark slickered-back hair brushed tight to his scalp, sallow, droopy face more agitated than usual.

'What the hell is going on in this town, Tully?' Tom demanded harshly as he approached the big, centrally placed desk behind which Mayor Tully sat.

'I'm sorry, sir, I couldn't stop him,'

the thin man cried out.

A second of startlement showed in the mayor's fat, hairless face, then it was gone.

'It's all right, Alfred,' Tully placated, then: 'Tom, I didn't expect to see you up and about so soon.'

'Seems to me that's what most folk think. Well I'm up, about an' ready to start work, an' my first job is to throw those two jokers in my office into jail.'

'Sir,' Alfred broke in unhappily, hovering behind and to the right of Tom.

'Leave us, Alfred. The sheriff an' I have some talking to do.'

'Sir,' Alfred Mason, Tully's secretary, murmured in relief. He almost ran for the door, pulling a white linen square from a pocket to mop his sweating brow.

'Sit down, Tom,' Tully invited, waving a thick-fingered hand towards a chair in front of the desk. His round face wore its professional smile. 'You seem to have made a remarkable recovery. The doctor opined that it would be a time yet before you were fit enough to work again.'

'Well, I'm ready now,' Tom said bluntly, refusing the offer of a seat and glaring sourly across the desk at Tully.

Mayor Tully returned the glare with an avuncular smile. Of medium height and with his round, full body and hearty manner, he had the appearance of everybody's favourite uncle. It was an appearance that he carefully nurtured and one that had kept him in office for more than twenty years. Behind him the back wall was decorated with a number of animal heads: deer, elk, mountain lion, bear.

'Sit yourself down, Tom,' he said gently. 'You look a mite beat.'

'Nokes seems to think the job of sheriff is his for good,' Tom said, still ignoring the offer of a seat even though his legs cried out for a rest.

The smile slid a little on Tully's face. 'You've spoken to Nokes?' His words came out more sharply than he intended.

'I went to my office first.'

'You should have come straight to me,' Tully pointed out.

'Well, is it true?' Tom demanded.

'Can I get you a drink, Tom? Coffee, tea, whiskey?'

'All I want is answers.'

Mayor Tully sighed and reached forward to a wooden, ornately carved humidor which sat on his desk and opened it.

'Cigar?'

'Who is the sherrif in this town?' Tom persisted.

Tully selected a cigar and closed the lid.

'You sure do have a one-track mind this morning.'

'All I want is the answer to a simple question. You owe me that much.' Tom was getting impatient and it showed in his voice, but Tully was not a man to be rushed. For the next few minutes he applied himself to preparing the cigar and only when it was lit did he speak again.

'A town like this needs a lawman to keep the peace.'

'It's what I've been doing for the last five years.'

'An' mighty grateful we are for that. Like I told the town council, ain't another man can stand in your shadow, but . . . ' He shrugged apologetically.

'But what?'

'Look at yourself, Tom. You got one good arm. How you gonna stand up to a saloonful o' drunken cowhands on a Saturday night. A town needs a lawman wi' two good arms.'

'It'll mend,' Tom cut back.

'Mebbe, mebbe not. That shoulder o' yours is busted up pretty bad. From what Doc says it may never mend properly. Could be you'll never get the full use o' that arm back agin. It's your gun arm, Tom. You were the fastest draw I'd seen in a long time an' it was fear o' that draw that kept the law-breakers outta town. Wi' that shoulder busted up you've lost that edge.' Tully shrugged regretfully.

'An' you reckon the likes of Nokes and Colson will be able to stop them?' Tom felt like laughing. 'Why in tarnation did the town council elect those two clowns?' He glared suspiciously at Tully. 'Or mebbe they were pushed a little, eh, Mayor, considering they ride line for you on that spread o' yours?'

Mayor Tully jetted a stream of smoke.

'I can see you must be feeling cheated an' it's a pity you didn't come an' see me first.'

'Would that have changed things any?' Tom shot back bitterly.

'Mebbe not,' Tully conceded, 'but it would have put you in a better frame o' mind to hear me out.'

'I'm listening.'

'Then let's hope you're hearing. That busted-up shoulder finishes you as a lawman, but it just so happens that I'm in need of a ranch manager. Oversee the hands, keep the books, that sorta thing. It's a job that don' worry 'bout a busted shoulder. I reckon you can handle it. How'd you feel 'bout it? An' afore you answer, it pays more than being a sheriff an' getting yoursel' shot at by drunken cowhands. What do you say?'

Tom studied the florid, smiling face of the mayor wreathed in a haze of cigar smoke.

'I say you can keep your job, Tully. I wasn't born to sit behind no desk.'

Mayor Tully's smile faltered a little and he shrugged.

'You're still a mite upset, I can understand that. I tell you what, you think on it a spell an' let me know by the end o' the week. Like I said afore, the town's beholden to you for the fine job you did in keeping the law an' that's why town funds are paying for your hotel room an' all the doctoring fees.' His voice took on an ominous tone and his face hardened. 'But it cain't last for ever. Think 'bout my offer, Tom, an' you'll see the sense of it.' Their eyes locked for an instant, then his tone brightened. 'The ranch can do wi' a good man like you to run it an' it'll sure take a load off my shoulders.'

'Let me know how much I owe the town funds. I pay my own way,' Tom said brusquely. With that he turned away and headed for the door.

Mayor Tully watched him go. Only when the door slammed shut and he was on his own did the smile fade and a hard, cold glitter fill his eyes. Here was the real Edward Tully that hid behind the jovial, back-slapping mayor: a hard, ruthless man who did not like his empire rocked. Just now Tom Morgan was shaking it a little.

Nokes and Colson were lounging outside the sheriff's office when Tom emerged. As he approached Nokes stepped out in front of him, thumbs hooked in his gunbelt.

'What did the mayor say, Sheriff?' Nokes laid emphasis on the final word turning it into a taunt.

'Get outta my way, Nokes,' Tom said brusquely.

'Let me guess,' Nokes continued. 'He said you were finished being a sheriff in Prospect an' now I'm the official, duly appointed law in town. That makes you an ordinary citizen. Now ain't that a crying shame, Mr Nobody.' Behind Tom, Colson chuckled out loud.

'Mr Nobody, I surely do like that.'

Nokes thrust his face close to Tom's.

'That means in future you call me Sheriff Nokes or Mr Nokes, boy. Got me a few nights in jail to settle wi' you so I'll be watching you real close.' Nokes stepped back grinning at Tom's angry, tight-lipped face. 'Reckon just now you'd like to take a swing at me eh, boy? Why don't you try? You still got one good arm.'

Tom fought to keep his anger under control.

'Happen there'll come a time when I'll take you up on that, Nokes.' It was Tom's turn to lay emphasis on the name without any form of title before it and was rewarded to see Nokes's face darken.

Nokes took a threatening step forward and thrust his face close to Tom's.

'Happen I'll look forward to that time, Morgan,' he grated, his rancid breath filling Tom's nostrils. 'Now git on or I'll throw you in jail for causing a breach o' the peace . . . my peace.' He stepped aside.

Tom gave him a wintry stare, looked as though he was about to say something, shook his head and continued his interrupted journey, aware that the two men were laughing at him.

In his office, Mayor Tully had witnessed the exchange of words between the two from his window. He had not heard what was said, but he was in no doubt that Nokes was goading Morgan. It was a situation Mayor Tully wished to avoid. Tom Morgan was still a popular figure about town and by the looks Nokes received from passers-by, they did not like the way the new sheriff was treating Tom. It was something he, Tully, would have to put a stop to.

Tom returned to his hotel room and slumped tiredly on the creaking, brass-framed bed. The morning's encounters had drained him physically and mentally. He couldn't understand what was going on or why.

Gingerly he eased his arm from the sling. The damaged shoulder protested, but he ignored the twinges of pain. He stood up and gently rotated his shoulder. The twinges became red-hot stabbing knives that brought a bubbling cry to his lips, ending in a throaty curse. He returned the arm to the support of the sling.

It would take time to heal. In the meantime, he could find out a little more about the lost patrol and perhaps give some meaning to Ethan Small's death and to that of the Blakes. He lay back on the bed and let the warmth of the day cocoon him in a web of drowsiness.

3

The following morning Tom rode north out of Prospect, heading towards the rugged foothills of the Guadalupe Mountains. El Paso lay a hundred miles to the west, Pecos a similar distance to the east. Beyond the grey ridge of the Guadalupes lay New Mexico. Protected by the mountains and nurtured by its streams, the area around Prospect was a lush, green oasis surrounded by a more arid landscape.

Away from town Tom felt good and breathed the warm, sweet air contentedly. He had discarded the sling and even though his shoulder ached he felt better without it.

An hour from town found him approaching the cabin that had once belonged to Ethan Small. An old Indian, dressed in Western-style clothes, watched his approach. The seamed and wrinkled leather of his ancient face showed no emotion. Hair once black was now white, pulled back severely and tied in a tail that reached down between his shoulder blades. For all his age, the powerful build of his youth still remained in his broad shoulders.

Tom smiled as he approached the man.

'Hi, George, is Miss Emma home?'

Lakota George nodded his head briefly. At that moment the door of the cabin opened and Emma Small emerged onto the wooden veranda boards creaking beneath her feet. She paused at the top of the step.

Clad in black boots, blue Levis, a red-check shirt and leather vest that matched the colour of the boots, the mannish garb failed to hide the woman beneath. Chestnut-coloured hair tumbled about her slim, pretty face, falling to her shoulders.

Tom felt a surge in his breast at the sight of her. He swept the hat from his head and smiled at her, but the smile was not returned. Her face remained wooden, brown eyes expressionless.

'What do you want here, Sheriff? I'm rather busy.' The tone of her voice erased the welcoming smile from his face.

'I came by to see how you are an' offer my condolences for your pa. I'm real sorry for what happened. Your pa saved my life.'

'It's a pity there was no one around to save his,' she retorted sharply.

Her words stung him. Before the business with her pa he had been getting on pretty good with her, taking her out on a picnic on two occasions. Now it was like they had never met. He felt suddenly confused.

'I'm sorry, Emma,' he mumbled weakly again.

'So am I, Sheriff. I thought you were his friend, but I guess not. Now please leave, you are not welcome here.'

The words stabbed at him like a knife and he floundered in a sea of bewildered misery, searching for words to say to bridge the rift that had opened before them and finding none. He had words for tears and anger, but not this cold, emotionless display. He could have said he was only doing his job, but it didn't seem the right moment or the right thing to say.

'I'm not the sheriff any more,' he temporized.

For a brief moment his words brought a thin, ugly sneer to her lips.

'After doing their dirty work, your town friends have now discarded you. Rough justice, but at least you are alive. Now please leave and stay off my land. There is nothing more to say.' Her voice was faltering, breaking up as the barrier she had built began to fall apart. 'Please see the ex-sheriff off my land, George.' She turned away and stumbled back into the cabin slamming the door behind her.

Tom released pent-up breath in a hiss. The day had suddenly lost its warmth and brightness in the face of her hostility and anger. He slowly replaced his hat and shook his head, disconcerted and lost. He turned his head as Lakota George took a step forward.

'I'm on my way, George,' he said miserably, but the old Indian held up a hand.

'She is full of hurt and anger,' he said.

'I guess that makes two of us,' Tom replied.

'It was a bad thing they did.'

'I'm sorry Ethan died,' Tom began, but the old man silenced him with a shake of his head.

'Death is part of life, the two go hand in hand,' Lakota George dismissed. 'It was what they did afterwards.'

Tom stared into the seamed, leather face.

'I'm not sure I understand,' he said uncertainly.

'They would not lay him in the white man's burial ground. Instead they brought the body of Ethan Small here, and left him on the ground. Together we buried him.'

Tom stared down at the upturned face, a growing look of horror twisting his bearded features into a mask of outrage.

'Oh, my God?' he breathed, then his voice hardened. 'Who did this?'

'It was the one who now wears the star and his deputy.'

'Then Tully must have ordered it,' Tom grated. 'Thanks for telling me, George.'

'You are a good man. She needs such as you to help her,' Lakota George said simply.

'I don' think she shares your views, George,' Tom said sadly, 'but I'll be here when . . . if she needs me.' Tom touched the brim of his hat to the old Indian, wheeled his horse and headed back to town, a grim expression on his face.

★　★　★

'I've heard an' seen a lotta things, Tully, but not allowing a man a decent burial just about beats them all.' The anger that had been brewing inside Tom on his journey back to town finally erupted as he faced Mayor Tully, heedless of the other four men seated around the desk.

Through a haze of cigar smoke Tully glared hard at Tom.

'This is the second time you've come into my office without being asked, Morgan, an' it sure as hell's gonna be the last. This here's a private council meeting an' you ain't invited. Now git out afore I have you thrown out,' he thundered.

Tom felt four other pairs of eyes on him. He recognized the others around the table. Chuck Clayton, the burly, thick-shouldered owner of the saloon. Ben Trimble, who ran the dry-goods store, Bart Lorimer, the fat banker, and Seth Haggerman, owner of the general store. They all waited for Tom's reaction, filled whiskey glasses temporarily forgotten.

'A man deserves more than to be dumped like a piece of meat at the feet of his daughter,' Tom shot back.

'An' what about the people he butchered?' Tully returned.

'Alleged butchered. It was not proved in a court o' law.'

'That's 'cause he went on the run.' Chuck Clayton spoke up. 'That's proof enough for me that he was guilty.' Lorimer and Ben Trimble nodded vigorous agreement with Clayton's words while Seth Haggerman stared fixedly at a spot on the desk between his hands and remained silent.

'He went on the run in the hope that he could find the killers responsible,' Tom replied.

'And how do you know that?' Tully enquired.

'Because he told me an' I'm inclined to believe him,' Tom returned hotly.

'An' what else did he tell you?' Tully raised his eyebrows.

'Enough to make me think he might have been innocent.'

Tully smiled. 'You always did come out on the side of the underdog, Tom, giving them the benefit of the doubt, an' you were kinda sweet on his daughter too, so I hear.'

'What the hell's that got to do with it?' Tom asked angrily.

'You tell me, but if I was you I'd keep ideas that Small was innocent to myself. Feelings are running pretty high. The Blakes were well liked. Could be if'n it got out folks might get a little worked up 'bout it. All the evidence pointed to Small. My advice to you is to let it lie. The Blakes are dead an' their killer, Ethan Small, is dead too. The matter is closed.' Heads around the table nodded.

'Except for one thing,' Tom said tautly.

'That is?' Tully prompted.

'Why would Ethan Small have killed them. They were neighbours and friends. There was no reason.'

'What reason would anyone else have to kill them?' Tully returned.

44

'Blake was looking into what happened to the lost patrol and the gold they were supposed to be carrying.' Tom paused, letting his eyes drift over the four men. 'Maybe he found out.' With that he turned on his heel and marched out of the room.

Outside, Tom's shoulders sagged a little as the tension and anger of the moment drained away. He massaged the top of his right arm, which had begun to ache.

'You'd better let me take a look at that.'

Tom turned at the sound of Doc Maddison's voice. The little doctor in his brown suit, old battered hat and ever-present bag approached along the sidewalk, his face etched in a perpetual scowl.

'It's fine, Doc,' Tom protested, causing the scowl on the other's face to deepen.

'Damn patients think they know best. I'm the doctor around here an' I'll tell you if'n it's fine or not.'

Ten minutes later Tom, shirt off, winced as Doc Maddison manipulated his shoulder in the quiet confines of his small surgery.

'OK, it aches a bit,' Tom said.

'That's 'cause you took it outta the sling too damn soon,' Doc grumbled. He examined the area of the wound. 'Healing up fine, but if'n you don't rest that arm an' give the damaged muscles inside a chance to heal, you ain't never gonna get back the full use of it.' He straightened and glared at Tom as he pulled his shirt on. 'Another week an' mebbe you can start giving it some gentle exercise.'

'I'll keep it rested, Doc,' Tom promised.

'An' mebbe pigs can fly,' Doc growled.

Tom's bearded lips twitched in a smile, then a thoughtful look settled in his eyes.

'What's happened to this town, Doc, that they'd refuse a man a decent burial?'

Doc twitched an eyebrow as he looked at Tom.

'If'n you're referring to Ethan Small, as I reckon you are, then you gotta remember they'd just buried the Blakes, butchered by Small, an' they weren't 'bout to have his killer lying alongside them. Let his own take care o' him.'

'That's mighty Christian of them,' Tom replied, his voice heavy with sarcasm.

'Yeah. Like it was a Christian thing he did to the Blakes,' Doc cut back.

'Convicted and found guilty without a trial,' Tom sneered.

'He broke jail and ran. To most folks' minds that adds up to guilty,' Doc pointed out hotly, echoing Chuck Clayton's words of earlier. 'Add that to the evidence that was already agin him. I reckon that's pretty conclusive.'

'Evidence that don't sit right wi' me,' Tom brooded.

Doc's eyes narrowed as they looked at him.

'It was clear enough.'

'Too clear. Think on it, Doc. What sort o' killer leaves his own, instantly recognizable, knife in his victim's body then hides a bloodstained shirt in his own barn to be easily found? Then the victim manages to write the name of his killer using his own blood before he dies. How convenient.' Sarcasm dripped from his words.

'What in tarnation are you trying to say, Tom?'

'That Ethan didn't kill the Blakes, but someone sure wanted it to look that way.'

Doc Maddison shook his head and shrugged

'Guess it don' make no difference now. The Blakes are gone, Small's gone.'

'Oh but it does, Doc. Whoever killed the Blakes and left Ethan Small to take the blame is still out there. I intend to find out who it was,' Tom said grimly.

'Seems a mighty tall order for one man.'

Tom smiled tautly.

'Gotta do somethin' while my shoulder's a-mending.'

Doc Maddison eyed the younger man with troubled eyes.

'Let it rest, Tom. Ain't nothing gonna bring the Blakes or Small back.'

'I still believe in justice, Doc. There's a girl a-hurting over what they say her pa did. It don' sit right wi' me to see her suffer while the real killers or killer get away with it.'

Doc snorted and squinted at Tom's determined face. 'An' just how do you propose to perform this miracle when all parties concerned are dead?'

'I'm working on it, Doc,' Tom parried.

'An' what if'n it turns out that Small did kill them?'

'The truth is all I'm after.'

'You realize that if'n you go poking about in something that most folks see as settled to their satisfaction you could stir up a lotta trouble that'll be aimed right at you?'

'If'n it stirs up the real killers it'll be

worth it,' Tom replied. He settled his hat on his head and headed for the door, where he paused and looked back at Doc. 'Ethan Small was a big man, but so was Jed Blake an' Mrs Blake was no shrinking violet. How did Ethan Small manage to kill both of them with a knife an' not get so much as a bruise or a scratch? It ain't possible, Doc. An' why use a knife in the first place? A gun would have been easier.'

Doc shrugged. 'I'm just a man who fixes broken bones. You tell me why, you seem to have all the answers.'

'I don't yet but I fully intend to. But to my way o' figuring, a knife can be identified, a bullet can't. Something's going on here, Doc. Something that started fifteen years ago when, on a dark, stormy night, a wagon full of confederate gold rolled into town an' left a legend behind. Thanks for your time, Doc.'

With that enigmatic statement Tom left the surgery.

4

'The Lost Patrol. Why'd you wanna know 'bout the Patrol?' Jake Bundy peered aggressively at Tom, eyes glaring in his seamed and weathered, white whiskered face. The two stood in the warm gloom of the livery stable which was filled with the scent of hay and horse-droppings. The big doors at either end of the stable were open, but the daylight never quite reached the middle of the long aisle that ran between the rows of horse-boxes, deserted while their occupants were grazing in an outside corral. Above the horse-boxes the open-fronted haylofts were piled to the roofs with hay.

Tom had found Jake mucking out a horse-box near the far end where sunlight angled cautiously in a white bar through the open door. Jake Bundy had been the stage-driver that fateful

51

day and this was the first time since then that Tom had seen him.

'Heard you was up an' about,' Jake had greeted him. 'Thought at one time you weren't gonna make it.'

'Without your help mebbe I wouldn't have. I'm obliged to you, Jake.'

'I'd'a come a-visiting, but I weren't sure if'n you wanted to see me. Called me a damn fool for shooting that killer.' There had been a baleful note in the old man's voice, a defensive edge. Tom did not try to correct the other in describing Ethan Small as a killer. He was after information, not aggression.

'I ain't blaming you, Jake. Reckon I'd've done the same in your boots,' Tom had replied and this had chirped the old man up.

'Reckon any man would've,' Jake agreed, nodding, the defensive manner melting away until Tom mentioned the Lost Patrol and then it was back again.

'Why'd you wanna hear that?' He scowled at Tom. 'Reckon everyone in Prospect knows the story anyhow.'

'I'd just like to hear it the way it was an' figured you was the one to tell it, seeing as how you were here at the time.'

'More'n half the folks in Prospect today were here then,' Jake pointed out.

'Hell, Jake, if'n you're gonna be that prickly 'bout it then I'll go an' find someone else,' Tom returned.

'Ain't prickly,' Jake defended. 'Must'a tol' it a thousand times since it happened. Guess I'm all talked out 'bout it now.'

'Well, how about humouring me for old times' sake?' Tom prodded.

'Ain't gonna be no different from what you've heard already,' Jake pointed out.

'Mebbe not, but I ain't heard it from the horse's mouth, so to speak an' I weren't here when it happened.'

Jake shrugged and leaned the broom against the side of the stall.

'Why not. Got me some coffee a bubblin' out back that you're welcome to share.'

'Suits me,' Tom agreed and followed the old man outside and across to a small cabin that was Jake's home. The door was open as they approached it and inside Tom could see the outline of a pot-bellied stove, its smoke-pipe jutting from the sloping back roof.

Outside the hut a pair of old rockers were set either side of the door on the wooden decking shaded by the over-hang. Jake gestured for Tom to take a seat while he disappeared inside. He was back within minutes carrying two white tin mugs, the enamel on them chipped and pitted. Silently he handed one to Tom, saying nothing until he was comfortably seated.

Seated there, before the hut, they looked across the corral where half a dozen horses grazed contentedly.

'Ain't much to tell really,' Jake began. 'It was fifteen years ago in sixty-five. The war was near over. The Rebs were low on everything. Food, guns, bullets, men even, but General Lee weren't 'bout to give in, no sir.' Jake sniffed and paused to take a noisy sip of his coffee. 'You could say the gold the patrol was carrying was the Rebs' last chance. It was going to be used to buy guns and ammunition. I 'member well the day they rode into town. Driver an' a guard. Four men in the wagon, two on horseback.'

'Why'd they come to Prospect an' not another town?'

'They were heading across the Guadalupes into New Mexico where the guns were waiting for them. Eagle Pass was the only way over the mountains an' we were the last town they could git supplies from afore they hit Eagle Pass.'

'An' you gave 'em the supplies.'

'Dammit, boy, o' course we did. This part o' Texas was Confederate country an' proud of it.'

'So what happened after they got their supplies?'

'They rested up till sundown an' then left. The damn Yankees were driving deeper into Texas an' word was that they had got wind o' the gold an' were looking for it. That's the last we ever saw o' them. A storm blew up in the mountains that night, a real humdinger. A week later a man rode into Prospect. He had been waiting for the wagon, but it never turned up. Me an' some others from town went up through Eagle Pass looking for it, but there was nary a sign. The wagon, horses an' men jus' disappeared.'

'What do you think happened to them?'

Jake shrugged. 'Mebbe a Yankee patrol was waiting for them. Could be they were hit by a flash flood when the storm came. Mebbe they decided the war was a lost cause an' jus' kept on riding. Folks have searched for years believing the gold is still up there somewhere, but no one's ever found it.'

'Do you think it's still up there, Jake?'

'I did at one time, but it seems more'n likely them boys took off West. Utah, California, split it up between themselves an' are rich men some-where. The war ended a few weeks later an' that was it.'

Tom swallowed half his cupful.

'An' it was never found?'

'Not for the want o' trying. Yankee soldiers spent a year looking before they gave up. An' men have been looking ever since for what they termed the Lost Patrol.'

'Lost or mebbe they just didn't want to be found,' Tom replied. He drained his cup and stood up. 'Mighty fine java, Jake, 'preciate it an' the story.' He handed the mug to Jake.

'Come by agin any time, Tom,' Jake said.

'I'll do that, Jake,' Tom promised.

As he walked back on to Main Street he pondered on what to do next. The story of the lost patrol was much as he had heard before. One ugly possibility did cross his mind. Had Blake and Small found the gold and then argued over it? He dismissed the idea.

'Hear you bin causing trouble at the mayor's place.'

Tom came to a halt. He had been so engrossed in his own thoughts that he had not seen Hoyt Nokes blocking his path.

Nokes, thumbs hooked behind his belt-buckle, chuckled nastily and fixed his beady eyes on Tom.

'Is that a fact,' Tom replied casually.

'It's what I heard an' the mayor ain't too happy 'bout it.' A belligerent note crept into Nokes's voice.

'So what do you intend to do about it?' Tom asked.

Nokes's eyes narrowed. 'I 'tend to make sure it don' happen agin. You're riling the wrong folk, Morgan. If'n I was you I'd get outta town afore you end up doing a spell behind bars.'

'But you're not me an' I intend to be around for a long time yet,' Tom replied mildly. 'By the way, where's Colson? You got him stashed away somewhere close by with a rifle trained on me in case I turn nasty?'

Nokes's face reddened and he took half a step forward, jerking his thumbs from the belt-buckle and balling them into fists.

'I don' need no back-up to take you on, Morgan,' he grated.

Tom flicked his eyes around. A crowd had begun to gather. He settled his gaze on Nokes and raised his voice.

'You fixing to beat on an unarmed, injured man, Nokes?'

Nokes snapped a quick look at the silent, gathered people. He was well aware that his appointment as sheriff had not been welcomed by a lot of people in town and it showed in the hostile looks he was receiving.

'I'll be keepin' an eye on you, Morgan,' he hissed. 'Step outta line agin an' you'll end up in jail.' With that Nokes turned on his heel and marched away. Tom watched him go as the people round about began to disperse. One group of four headed by Seth Haggerman approached Tom.

'It ain't right that the likes of Nokes

and Colson should be allowed to run the law in Prospect,' Seth stated.

'You're on the town council, Seth. You hired them,' Tom said bluntly.

'I was out-voted three to one when the mayor put their names forward for office,' Seth said defensively.

'T'aint law, it's a damn farce,' Bill Rance, who worked in the barber's shop put in, with a disdainful sniff of his long bony nose.

'Can't figure why the rest o' the town council agreed to hiring 'em in the first place,' Joe Cutler muttered. He was the smallest of the four. A trim, dapper man who ran a gun store.

'Because they do what Tully tells them to do,' Seth replied bitterly.

'Much the same as Nokes an' Colson,' Moss Bailey, the local blacksmith, declared. He was the biggest of the four, clad in a spark-scarred leather apron, upper arms heavy with muscle. 'They only do what Tully tells them to do.'

'Do other folks feel the same way as

you?' Tom asked.

'Quite a few now,' Seth replied.

'We want you back as sheriff, Tom,' Joe Cutler said. 'This town's getting a bad reputation since them two jokers pinned on badges.'

'Mebbe I don't want it back. I heard what this town did with Ethan Small's body.'

'Now hold on, Tom, a lotta folks didn't agree wi' that,' Seth Haggerman said.

'Well, they should've disagreed louder,' Tom said thinly. 'Sorry, gents, but as it was once pointed out to me, a one-armed lawman is 'bout as useful as a three-legged hoss. Now if'n you'll excuse me, got business o' my own to deal with.' With that Tom turned on his heel and continued his interrupted journey.

It came as something of a revelation to learn that Tully was not as popular as he thought he was, but as Tom was soon to learn, Tully still ruled the roost. As he entered the hotel lobby to go to his room the manager, in his blue, store-bought suit, hurried forward and blocked his way to the stairs.

Sweat sheened Ed Stoppard's thin face and he rubbed his thin hands nervously together.

'I'm sorry, Mr Morgan, but you no longer have a room here. Your personal items have been packed.' He cast a nervous eye to a chair against one brown-painted wall. Tom followed his gaze and saw his old carpet-bag sitting on it. He turned his eyes back on the sweating manager.

'What in tarnation's going on here, Ed?' he demanded angrily.

Stoppard pulled forth a red-spotted kerchief and mopped his face.

'The town council are no longer paying for your room and I cain't afford to let you stay here free.'

'OK, I'll pay for it myself.'

'Oh, dear.' Stoppard swallowed nervously. 'I'm sorry, it's already taken.'

'Then I'll take another.'

'We're full up. I'm sorry.'

It was a lie and Tom knew it.

'No need apologizing to him, Stoppard. You heard the man, Morgan.'

Tom snapped his head around as Nokes, this time accompanied by Mitch Colson, appeared from a doorway beside the reception desk. Both were toting shotguns as they moved to a position before the desk.

'You sure do get about, Nokes,' Tom said mildly, keeping the anger that had flared through him under control. 'See you've brought your back-up with you this time. Mighty impressive agin an unarmed man.'

'You've gotta smart mouth, Morgan. One day it's gonna get you into real trouble.'

'You ain't gotta smart anything, Nokes, an' one day that's gonna get you into bigger trouble,' Tom retorted.

Nokes's face darkened. 'You jus' cain't stop pushing, can you, Morgan.' He growled softly. 'Well I'm a reasonable man. Town council's passed a new rule today. Drifters ain't welcome in

Prospect. You ain't gotta place to stay, you ain't gotta job an' that makes you a drifter. You got twenty-four hours to get outta town or I got the legal right to put a bullet in you. It's all in the new town charter.' Now it was Nokes's turn to smile. 'Please say you'll stay an' make me a happy man.' His smile widened even further. 'Your guns have been confiscated, drifters ain't allowed weapons in Prospect. You can pick 'em up when you leave.' He waited for a response, but Tom remained silent, face a stony mask.

'Figure the cat must'a got his tongue,' Mitch Colson piped up, grinning along with Nokes.

'That what it is, Morgan? Never thought I'd see the day when Tom Morgan's smart mouth was lost for words,' Nokes jeered.

Tom remained silent, not trusting what he would say once he started. Nokes was deliberately pushing him and now was not a good time to rise to the bait. He drew himself erect and forced a smile on lips that had nothing to smile about.

'Guess I'm no match for you, Nokes. I'll be in for my guns later.' With that apparent acknowledgement of defeat he grabbed up his carpet-bag and marched stiff-backed from the hotel, leaving a bewildered-looking Nokes staring after him.

5

Tom was seething inside.

A month ago he had been a respected lawman in Prospect, now he was without a job, without a home and classed as a drifter. His world had been turned upside down since the coach crash and Ethan Small's death.

He crossed Main Street heading towards Annie's, in need of a cup of hot, strong java and time to think. He paused outside Annie's long enough to rid himself of the sling before entering.

There was an enticing array of food-smells within that made his nose twitch and his mouth water. There were but a dozen tables inside, each covered with a sparkling white cloth. There was also a short counter along which were ranged six stools. Tom made his way to a corner table that over the years he had made his own and tossed his bag down irritably before slumping into a chair. From this position, back to the wall, he could survey the entire room.

Annie, a big, buxom lady in her mid-forties, clad in pink-check gingham overlaid with a white apron, greeted him happily. After fussing over him for a few minutes she brought him his coffee and left him on his own as more customers came in.

Left to his own thoughts he tried to remember back to when his world fell apart. It all came back to the moment when he had openly stated to Mayor Tully that he didn't believe Ethan Small killed the Blakes and he was going to try his hardest to prove it. That left the burning question: why was Tully so convinced of Small's guilt and so against an investigation to prove Small's innocence?

Annie had left him a coffee-pot and he poured himself a second cup as he mulled the question over in his mind. So deep was he in his thoughts that he didn't know he had a visitor until a shadow fell across him. He snapped his head up to find the person of his thoughts standing before him.

'Hello, Tom, I'm glad I found you. Mind if'n I sit a spell?' Mayor Tully beamed amiably down at him. 'Reckon we got some talking to do.'

'Excuse me if'n I find the first part a mite hard to swallow. Seems to me that I'd be the last person you'd want to speak to.'

'Mend a few bridges, so to speak,' Mayor Tully replied, taking Tom's words as an invitation to sit.

Intrigued despite himself, Tom sat back in his chair and waited for the other to explain himself. Tully ordered a pot of coffee. When it had arrived and he had poured himself a cup, he eyed Tom.

'Best damn coffee in Prospect,' Tully said with a smile.

'Is that what you came to tell me, Mayor?' Tom cocked an eyebrow.

Tully pulled a wry face.

'I'll allow we mebbe got off on the wrong foot,' he said in the closest approximation of an apology Tom had ever heard from the man. 'I can understand you felt bad to find Nokes had taken your job, but let's face it, Tom, with only one good arm, trying to uphold the law would have proved a tad foolish. There are a lotta hotheads around who, once the word got out, would be riding into Prospect looking to try you out.' Tully took a sip from his cup.

'So what exactly are you trying to say?' Tom prompted.

'That by giving Nokes the job I've probably saved your life. Dammit, Tom, you're too smart a fella to want to spend your days dodging bullets. Your gun arm's gone. Even when its mended you'll never be as quick as you was. The job of ranch manager I offered afore is still open to you. What do you say, Tom?' He eyed the bearded ex-lawman hopefully.

Tom returned the stare, his face

giving away nothing. First the iron fist, now the velvet glove. What was Tully up to?

'What if'n I say no?'

'That'd be a pure disappointment. The town charter still stands. Unless a man has a job an' a place to stay, he becomes a drifter an' that type o' man is not welcome in Prospect. We want folk who'll be a benefit to the town, not a liability. Drifters wi' time on their hands an' nothing to do tend to cause trouble an' we aim to avoid that happening here. Ain't saying you would, but there can be no exceptions to the rule.' Mayor Tully looked almost sorrowful. 'You understand what I'm saying, Tom?'

'Clear as a mountain lake, Mayor.'

'It's good we understand each other.' Mayor Tully nodded his silver head. 'So what do you say, Tom? Ranch manager o' the Circle T. Pays more'n sheriff's money.'

'My ol' pappy said to me to be polite and to say my thank yous to folks. Well, thank you, Mayor, but no thank you. I've got other plans.'

For the first time the smile on Mayor Tully's heavy face faltered and his eyes narrowed.

'Then I'll be sorry to see you go, Tom.'

It was Tom's turn to smile now.

'No need to be, Mayor, I ain't going anywhere.'

The smile now totally abandoned Mayor Tully's face and a hard glint slipped into his eyes.

'You know the alternatives,' he snapped. 'You upset a lotta folk when you sided with Ethan Small. Mebbe this town ain't safe for you any more.' He rose to his feet and looked down at Tom. 'Mebbe you ain't as smart as I figured.' With that Mayor Tully turned on his heel and marched, stiff-backed, out of the café.

Tom slumped back in his seat. 'Damn!' he muttered to himself and drained his coffee. He had no immediate plans for his future; he had just wanted to wipe that smug smile from Tully's face.

Well he had done that all right, now he had some hard thinking to do.

★ ★ ★

'Came in the bank an' withdrew all his money, close on two thousand dollars. Hadda let him have it, what else could I do?' It was two hours later when Bart Lorimer, the rotund banker, presented himself before Mayor Tully.

Lorimer was sweating, but then he always sweated in his three-piece suit, shirt-collar buttoned up so tight it looked to be strangling him. He nervously turned a hat in his pink, soft hands as he waited for Tully's reaction.

'Did he say why?' Tully lit a cigar.

'No, sir, Mayor. That Tom Morgan can be tight-lipped when he's a mind to. Didn't want no banker's draft, hadda be cash.' The banker nodded jerkily and Tully could have sworn he heard the rolls of fat around the man's buttoned-up neck squeak.

Tully jetted smoke in the direction of the bank manager, a frown of displeasure on his face.

'Do you know where he is now?'

'See'd him ride outta town a while back, heading north. Could be he was leaving.'

'Could be,' Tully agreed, but Morgan was not the type to give up so easily. He was up to something and that made Tully uneasy. 'Well, thanks for telling me, Bart.'

'Hadda let him have it,' Lorimer repeated, relief in his voice that Mayor Tully had taken it so well. 'Well, good riddance, I say, that he's gone after spreading them lies that Ethan Small didn't kill the Blakes. Upset a few folks that did. Mind, we all know why, him being sweet on Small's daughter an' all.' Lorimer gave a leering smile.

'Thanks agin, Bart, I'm sure you got important banking business to do.'

Lorimer nodded. 'Have indeed, Mayor. Must be on my way.'

After the banker had gone Tully wandered across to the window that looked down onto Main Street. He wondered where Morgan was now and what he was up to. Of one thing he was sure, he had not seen the last of the ex-lawman.

* * *

The following morning as Hoyt Nokes sat behind the desk in the sheriff's office shuffling through a pile of wanted dodgers, the door opened and Tom walked in. At a second, smaller desk angled in the corner by the door, Mitch Colson lounged in a tipped-back chair, feet up on the desk, ankles crossed. He appeared to be half-asleep until Tom walked in, then he uncoiled, feet and chair-legs crashing to the floor.

Nokes peered up as Tom came to a halt in front of the desk. For an instant startlement filled his face, then it dissolved into a nasty smile.

'Well lookee what the wind's blown

in,' he cried, tossing the dodgers aside and leaning back in the seat, hands dropping to his lap. 'Come to say good-bye, Morgan? Well that's real neighbourly o' you. Ain't that neighbourly, Mitch.'

'Sure is, Sheriff,' Mitch Colson agreed and Tom cast him a brief look, noting that the other had drawn his gun and was letting it rest on the desk top with his hand wrapped casually around it.

Tom looked back at Nokes.

'I've come to collect my guns, Nokes.'

'Sheriff Nokes,' Nokes pointed out, his smile fading to a glare.

'The guns, Nokes, I've got things to do.'

'That boy sure needs some respect taught him,' Mitch Colson called out.

'Perhaps a spell in jail will make him more respectful,' Nokes responded. He lifted his hand from his lap, fisting a Navy Colt that he placed gently on the desk top, but kept his hand on it. 'What d'yer say, Morgan?'

'I say you hand over my guns an' let me be on my way.'

'An' jus' why should I do that?'

Tom flourished a piece of paper.

'I now own the Weeping Rock gold mine, lock, stock an' barrel; that makes me a businessman an' not a drifter, so I'd be obliged if you'd hand over my guns.'

Nokes's jaw dropped as he snatched the deed from Tom's hand and studied it.

'You paid money to Clem Baker for a worthless, played-out claim?' There was disbelief in Nokes's voice.

'Legally witnessed and registered,' Tom agreed. 'As I'll be staying out at Weeping Rock I've got somewhere to stay an' a job, which, according to Lawyer Becker, means I've fulfilled all the requirements of the town charter. Now I'd like my guns please. Never can tell what wild animals might be roaming about there. Man needs to be armed.'

Nokes eyed him with narrowed eyes.

'What in damnation do you want with a played out mine, Morgan? You know it's worthless, Clem Baker knows it's worthless. Goddammit, everyone around here knows it's worthless so why would you throw good money away?'

Tom tapped the side of his nose with a finger.

'Let's just say I might know something that nobody else does an' leave it at that. The guns?'

'Well I ain't too sure 'bout that,' Nokes was still reluctant.

'Give him his weapons, Nokes and let him go.' It was Mayor Tully's voice that thundered out from behind causing Nokes and Colson to jump. Tom on the other hand just turned slowly, a smile on his face, and inclined his head towards Tully.

'That's mighty kind o' you, Mayor.'

Tully strode forward and stood before Tom.

'I don't know what you're up to,

Morgan, I figured you for a smart man, now it looks as though I was wrong.'

'Up to, Mayor?' Tom said with aggrieved innocence. 'I would have thought that was obvious.' He paused, turned, gathered up the weapons that Nokes had sullenly piled on the desk and turned back to Tully. 'I'm looking for gold an' something tells me that if'n I keep digging I'll find it.' There was a defiant challenge in his eyes as he spoke which Tully returned without expression. 'Now, if'n you'll excuse me, I've got work to do.' He brushed past the mayor and headed for the door, the man's eyes following every step he took.

'Mighty lonely out there for a man on his own,' he called as Tom reached the doorway. 'Man could fall, break a leg or worse an' nobody'd know.'

Tom paused and turned.

'I'll bear that in mind, Mayor,' he replied and disappeared out onto the sidewalk.

'Gonna need a long shovel to dig any gold outta that mine,' Colson chortled.

Tully snapped a look at the man and all his pent-up anger rushed to the fore.

'Shut up you damn fool!' he grated, then turned on Nokes. 'I want Morgan watched day and night. I want to know what he does, where he goes and who he talks to. Is that clear?'

'Ain't but the two o' us, Mayor. How we gonna do that an' look after the town?' Nokes cried in dismay.

'I don't care how you do it, Nokes, just make sure it's done an' I'm kept informed. Now's the time to earn the money I pay you. Make sure I'm not wasting that money or someone else will be sitting behind that desk. Do you understand what I am saying?'

'I understand, Mayor,' Nokes replied unhappily.

'Good.' Tully smiled unpleasantly. 'I'll expect to hear from you later today. An' keep this little arrangement to yourselves. No need letting the town know your business.' He turned on his heel and marched from the office, leaving the two bewildered men alone.

'Hell an' tarnation, what was all that about?' Colson asked. 'Mayor gotta burr in his pants?'

'Yeah, an' it's called Tom Morgan,' Nokes snapped. He glared across at Colson. 'Well, what are you waiting for, you heard the Mayor? Get on Morgan's tail an' stay there.'

'Why me?' Colson objected sullenly.

'Because I'm the sheriff an' you're the deputy. Now git on your horse an' find out what that ranny's up to!'

★ ★ ★

Tom rode out of town and headed north-west towards his newly acquired claim. It had been no accident that Tully had appeared in the sheriff's office when he did; Tom had engineered it. He knew Tully's routine. Every morning the mayor spent a while at his window, looking down on the town as it came alive, so he had waited until he knew Tully would be looking before putting in an appearance and then let the man's curiosity do the rest.

He had used Tully's own town charter to turn the tables on him, something that Tully would not like, but could do nothing about. It would gnaw at Tully like a rat at a carcass and maybe then the man would get careless. In the meantime it now gave him free range to pursue his own investigation, although what he was looking for and where to start he had no clear idea. For the moment he put the problem aside and enjoyed the ride.

It was a glorious morning. The sun shone from a cloudless sky falling across the towering Guadalope Mountains which spread along the northern border between west Texas and New Mexico. It was good cow country with plenty of lush grass nurtured by streams that tumbled from the high valleys of the mountains.

The land was flat to begin with, but as he drew nearer the grey flanks of the mountains the ground began to contort into deep valleys and high ridges fringed with tree and brush. He paused on one such ridge an hour later and looked down into a wide, fertile valley. From here he could see the cluster of buildings that made up Ethan Small's place and, a mile closer, almost hidden by a stand of beech, the silent, burnt-out remains of the Blake ranch. He climbed down from his horse and hunkered down in the shade of a straggling clump of chokecherry, tipping his hat back and peering down into the valley with thoughtful eyes.

Somewhere down there lay, if not the answer, then pieces of the puzzle that would lead to why the Blakes were murdered. All he had to do was find them.

Maybe Emma could supply a few answers, Ethan must have told her something or at least kept records, but the way she had made it clear he was not welcome on her land gave him little hope of her seeing him.

All in all his boast that he would get the real killer or killers of the Blakes was bravado rather than a realistic prospect. It would have been hard enough had he still been sheriff of Prospect and had the whole town behind him. As it was he had no one and everyone seemed to be against him.

He sighed, rose to his feet and returned to his horse and rode off the ridge, heading towards Weeping Rock.

6

Weeping Rock Canyon was a huge, horizontal cleft in one side of a narrow, canyon wall before the canyon opened into a circular, amphitheatre perhaps fifty feet across, ringed with high, sheer walls. The trail through the canyon was within the cleft itself so that the outward sloping wall became the roof as it curved overhead and all along its upper edge water dripped and trickled in a long, ragged glittering curtain.

The walls and floor of the cleft sparkled with water and the hoofs of Tom's horse clattered noisily within the cleft. The bottom of the canyon lay some ten feet below the cleft, choked with rock debris and brush.

The cleft ended as gradually the outward sloping cleft wall began to lift and straighten, eventually merging into the sheer wall of the canyon. The floor of the canyon lost its tortured, rock-strewn appearance and became a smooth, sandy track between the high walls that eventually opened into the rock ampitheatre that caught and held the heat of the day.

The walls were sheer, thrusting, ragged, sharp-toothed rims to the sky. To the right a thin curtain of water fell from an opening in the rock face tumbling fifty feet into a wide pool which in turn emptied into a narrow stream that ran for ten feet before disappearing underground.

Around the pool and along the stream, trees and brush had sprung up through a carpet of grass, forming a tiny, green oasis in an otherwise barren, stone-and-sand box canyon.

The Weeping Rock mine lay straight ahead: a dark, square hole in the rock face, framed with rough timber. Just before that a small, ramshackle log cabin squatted tiredly on the hard ground. Tom brought his mount to a halt in front of the cabin and slid from the saddle. The horse snickered and tossed its head in the direction of the water. Tom rubbed its muzzle, then, after removing saddle and reins let the horse follow its nose to the water and grass.

Tom dumped the saddle by the door of the cabin, threw the saddlebags over one shoulder and with his carpet-bag in one hand entered his new home through a hinge-groaning door. Apart from the door, a shuttered window next to it provided the only other means for light to enter the cabin. After depositing his bags Tom threw the shutters open. Light streamed through the glassless square to illuminate the sparse furnishings. These consisted of a bed against one wall, a table, chair and pot-belly stove. Beneath his feet the worn boards creaked in protest.

Tom let his gaze drift around, a faint smile on his face. It was a roof over his head and a base to work from and that was all he wanted. With a little bit of work it could be quite cosy.

He spent the rest of the day getting the cabin into some sort of order. By nightfall the stove had been fired up and a pot of coffee filled the tiny dwelling with a rich, aromatic smell. Old Clem had left him a glass-bodied storm-lantern and a half full can of kerosene. As darkness filled the canyon the lantern filled the cabin with a soft, yellow light.

Tomorrow he would go into town and stock up on supplies, but for now he was content to dine on cornbread biscuits and coffee and ponder his next move.

$\star$ $\star$ $\star$

Tom was up early the next morning and headed into town. His first stop was the hash-house on Main Street where he breakfasted on thick bacon slices, eggs and cornbread washed down with two cups of coffee. He had taken a table by the curtained window and as he waited for his breakfast to arrive, the lone figure of Mitch Colson appeared from the direction Tom had come. The man looked cold and miserable, shoulders hunched in his jacket.

A smile touched Tom's lips. He was sure someone had followed him from town yesterday and had a pretty shrewd idea it had been Colson. Tully would have wanted an eye kept on him and Nokes would have passed that little chore on to Colson.

As Tom's breakfast arrived Colson, stiff and cold, stamped into the sheriff's office. He made straight for the coffee-pot on the stove where, with shaking hands, he poured coffee into a tin mug.

'Well?' Nokes demanded.

'Well what?' Colson snapped back, hands around the mug to absorb a little heat.

'What did he do?'

'Stayed in that damn canyon all night while I froze my butt outside,' Colson replied sourly. 'He rode back into town this morning.'

'Is that all. The mayor ain't gonna be to pleased with that.'

'Then the mayor can go an' freeze his own butt off an' keep watch,' Colson returned sulkily. He gulped at the mug.

Tom ate a leisurely breakfast, then headed for the general store to get his supplies. A number of people were standing outside gawping when he rode up. He slid from his horse and hitched it to the rail a few yards down from a small buckboard he recognized as belonging to Emma Small. Lakota George sat wooden-faced on the driving seat. Seth Haggerman, the store owner, stood by the buckboard engaged in a heated argument with Nokes and Colson.

'What's going on, Stan?' Tom approached a small man on the edge of the crowd.

The man looked up and a smile cracked his thin, sallow face.

'Morning, Tom. Say, I hear you've turned goldminer?' he greeted cordially.

'You could say that,' Tom replied with

a smile. 'So, what's going on?'

'Somethin' to do wi' that Indian who works at the Small ranch. Causing trouble.'

Tom frowned. He knew Lakota George and the man was no trouble-maker. Nodding his thanks to Stan he pushed his way through the crowd to the front.

'I told you. George is welcome in my store an' I ain't having the likes o' you telling me who I can serve an' who I can't,' Seth Haggerman declared heatedly.

'Ain't too sure I like your tone o' voice, storekeeper,' Nokes growled, glaring at Seth.

'Reckon he's causing a breach o' the peace,' Mitch Colson added, grinning.

'And I don't like being told how to run my store,' Seth argued back hotly. There was a sheen of sweat on his thin face which told Tom he was not enjoying the encounter with Nokes and Colson. Tom broke from the crowd and strode towards the three.

'You got trouble here, Seth?' Tom asked mildly.

A look of relief flooded across Seth Haggerman's face as he looked at Tom.

'These damn fools are telling me that I can't serve George,' Seth fumed.

Tom turned his gaze on Nokes and Colson.

'Now why would that be?'

'This is none o' your business, Morgan, unless you wanna spend some time in jail.'

Tom smiled thinly.

'Well I'm making it my business.'

'He says it's a new town rule. No Injuns to be served, by order o' the town council. I'm on the town council an' I ain't heard of such a rule,' Seth raged.

'They sure do like making up rules,' Tom mused.

'An' I aim to keep 'em,' Nokes stated flatly. 'No Injuns.'

'An' no goddam Injun-lovers,' someone called from the crowd and received a buzz of approval.

Tom's eyes flickered to the assembled men. The ones backing up Nokes were from the saloon. Men with nothing to do but while away the time with a bottle: drifters.

'I thought there was a rule agin drifters with no work?' Tom returned his gaze to Nokes. The other shifted uncomfortably as a section of the growing crowd, made up of regular townsfolk, voiced their approval at Tom's words.

'Keep it up, Morgan. It'll sure pleasure me to throw you in jail.'

Tom ignored him and instead settled his gaze on Colson, a smile tugging at his lips.

'Cold night last night, Mitch, but I was real snug an' warm in my cabin. Sure wouldn't have liked spending a night outside, though.'

Mitch Colson stared sullenly at Tom, fury flaring in his eyes at the other's taunting smile.

'Don't know what you're gabbing about,' Mitch said thickly.

'Morgan, you sure are trying my patience,' Nokes broke in. 'Reckon that's earned you an' the Injun some jail-time. Breach o' the peace, I call it. Now you gonna come along quietly or with a bellyful o' buckshot?' He smirked and the crowd went quiet except for the shuffling of feet as those behind Tom moved out of the line of fire.

Tom smiled.

'Breach o' the peace. Them's fine sheriffing words, Nokes, mighty fine, yes sir.' He nodded in appreciation. While he had been speaking his fingers had slipped undone two buttons on his coat, now the coat fell open to reveal a holstered gun slung low on his left hip and tied into position about his left thigh. 'And in answer to your question, no I ain't coming quietly or otherwise.' The smile had left his face and his bearded features had become hard. 'Now if'n you think you can bring that cannon into play afore I put a bullet in your head, then make your move.' He elbowed the left side of the coat back and let his hand hang close to the butt of his gun.

Nokes stared at him in surprise.

'You're a right hand gun,' he blurted out.

A thin, cold smile touched Tom's lips, but failed to reach his eyes.

'Was deputy to a sheriff down Amarillo way. He was an old man an' you don't get to be an old man in the sheriff business unless you're good, an' I asked him one time how he got to be an old sheriff. 'Son,' he said, always called me son. 'If'n you wanna stay alive in this business then don't keep your eggs all in one basket, 'cause sure as dogs chase cats, one day you'll drop that basket an' like as not break all the eggs an' then you'll have none. Allus carry them in two baskets an' if'n one gets dropped you've got the other left'.' Tom paused, his eyes flickering from Colson to Nokes and back again.

'Eggs? What in tarnation are you

talking about, Morgan?' Nokes demanded hoarsely.

'Had me puzzled at first until he explained it to me. Think of your arms as being two baskets of eggs. One gets broke an' if'n that one is the one you use for pulling iron, then you've got real trouble, but you've got your other basket of eggs.' Tom paused again and Nokes looked more puzzled than he had before. Tom shook his head. 'What he was saying was, learn to use your other hand to pull iron until you're as fast with both. I put in a lot o' time an' practice drawing with my left hand until I was as fast at drawing and shooting with it as I was with my right.'

There was a gasp from the assembled onlookers.

'He's bluffing,' Mitch Colson said. 'I ain't never seen him use his left hand.'

'Never had the need to until now,' Tom said casually.

'Take him, Sheriff, call his bluff,' Colson urged.

Nokes turned on his deputy.

'Shut your damn face, Colson,' he snapped. There was a beading of sweat on Nokes's face. Morgan was too damn casual and confident to be bluffing.

'Tell you what, Mitch,' Tom called amiably. 'How 'bout you going for your gun. Sure would put the sheriff's mind at rest to find out if'n I'm bluffing or not.'

It was Colson's turn to look uneasy now as he became the centre of attention.

'Yeah, why don' you take him on, Colson?' someone from the crowd of onlookers called out, increasing the man's discomfort.

'Go ahead, Colson,' Nokes said softly.

Mitch Colson raised his hands to chest level before him.

'I ain't no gunfighter, never said I was,' he replied, bringing a jeer from the crowd.

'But he's jus' bluffing,' Nokes pointed out. 'That's what you said.'

Colson was saved any further embarrassment as Mayor Tully pushed his way through the crowd.

'What in tarnation's going on here?' he demanded.

Seth Haggerman stepped forward. 'Nokes is telling me I can't serve Lakota George. Orders from the town council. How come I ain't heard o' this order? What's going on, Tully.' It was significant that Seth had dropped the 'mayor' title, something that was not lost on Tully.

'Morgan here threatened us while we were doing our lawful duty,' Nokes cut in sullenly.

'Said he was a fast draw with his left hand,' Colson put in lamely.

Tully eyed Morgan.

'Seems like you can't keep outta trouble, Tom.'

'He weren't causing no trouble,' a voice called out from the crowd. 'Seth wanted to serve Lakota George an' Nokes said he couldn't; that ain't right. George is part of this town. He's been here longer than most. He only came in for supplies. I say he should have 'em.' There was a murmur of approval following these words.

Tully's eyes flickered around, noting the disapproval on the faces of those around and thought quickly. He sensed the mood of the crowd and saw an opening to maintain his standing with them.

'Seems to me there's been a misunderstanding here,' he said loudly. 'I see no reason not to serve George with what he wants, Seth.'

Nokes's eyebrows seemed to crawl up his forehead in surprise.

'But you said . . . ' he began hotly and stopped as Tully glared darkly at him before turning a smiling, apologetic face to the incensed Seth Haggerman.

'Sorry, Seth. There was an emergency council meeting last night an' we couldn't get hold of you.'

'Yeah, I was out visiting my folks over at Boulder Creek,' Seth supplied.

'Hadda message there was some 'breeds getting likkered up an' causing trouble in the next county. It was them I was talking 'bout. George here is one o' us, ain't that right, folks?' He smiled around.

'That's right, Mayor,' a voice called.

Tully gave a smile at the crowd and turned to Seth.

'You make sure you serve George with whatever he wants, an',' here he raised his voice so all could hear, 'you be sure an' charge it all to me.' There was a spontaneous outburst of clapping from the gathered crowd which was music to Tully's ears. The smile slipped from his face as his gaze fell on Nokes and Colson. 'Ain't no need for you two to be here, there is no problem, so be 'bout your business.'

'But Morgan here braced the sheriff,' Colson objected.

Tully's face darkened. He took a step towards the two as the crowd broke up.

'Are you hard o' hearing, Colson?' he snapped harshly. 'Get back to the office now, the pair o' you, I'll be dropping by later.'

Colson looked as though he was about to say something else, but Nokes caught his arm.

'We're going, Mayor, like you said, a misunderstanding.' He turned Colson and steered him away.

Tully turned around and faced Tom who had been watching and listening with an amused smile on his face.

'How does a miner's life suit you, Tom?'

'Early days yet, Mayor, but so far it's fine. I aim to start digging soon and who knows what I'll come up with.' He stared hard at Tully and the man reddened, the innuendo not lost on him. To cover his discomfort he turned to Lakota George.

'Sorry 'bout that, George, but you'll have no trouble in the future.' Lakota George stared impassively at Tully but said nothing.

Tully cleared his throat noisily.

'Well, other business to attend to.' He turned on his heel and almost scampered away from the store.

7

Cigar smoke hung heavy in the air of the sheriff's office. Mayor Tully sat at the sheriff's desk while Nokes and Colson stood the other side like a pair of naughty children who had been caught stealing apples. No longer needing to wear the amiable, avuncular face he presented to the public, Tully's face beneath the swath of white hair had become ugly and hard as he stared ferociously at the two.

'You two seem to have made it a habit to make fools of yourselves in public an' I'm getting real tired of having to drag your sorry butts outta the mud, so let's get a few things straight.' He leaned forward on the desk. 'Before Tom Morgan gathers more sympathy from your stupid actions, I want him taken care of, is that understood?'

Nokes shifted uneasily.

'That mebbe won't be so easy, Mayor,' he began and jumped as Tully's left hand banged angrily on the desk top.

'Don't let me have to call in outside help, Nokes,' Tully hissed, 'or mebbe that outside help will have two extra to deal with. Tom Morgan is one man, on his own out in the middle of nowhere. Accidents can so easily happen. Why, that ol' mine could easily cave in on him. If'n he had a bullet or two in him beforehand, ain't no one gonna know, 'cause no one's gonna try an dig him out. Do you get my meaning?'

'We get it, Mayor,' Colson piped up with a smile.

'How 'bout you, Nokes?'

'We can take care of him,' Nokes asserted, nodding.

'That's good, that's jus' what I wanted to hear, an' the sooner I hear it's all been taken care of the happier I'll be.' Tully nodded and blew smoke in the direction of the two before rising to his feet. 'I'll leave you gentlemen to get on with the business in hand. Don't let me down.' He picked up his hat and settled it on his head. At the door he paused to fix his smiling, public face in position before stepping out onto the sidewalk.

Later on in the day he had cause to smile even more when Bart Lorimer, the banker, paid him a visit.

'Are you sure she can't pay?' Tully questioned as he laid aside the document Lorimer had brought him.

'No, sir, Mayor. All the money he had went on stock. No way can she cover the outstanding amount.'

'Thank you, Bart, I'm beholden to you. Tomorrow we'll pay a neighbourly visit to Miss Small.'

Later, after the banker had departed, Tully poured himself a large whiskey and sipped it contentedly. Everything was starting to fall into place in his favour and that made him feel a whole lot better.

* * *

Before heading back to his new home Tom stopped off to speak to Jake Bundy. He found the grizzled livery-stable owner firing off at a frightened youngster who was in the middle of cleaning out the stalls.

'Dammit, boy, you ain't got the sense you wus born with. I said to leave the hay bales in that stall. I always keeps that stall filled. Now you get 'em back in there pronto, then get to clean out the rest o' the stalls.' He looked up as Tom's boots rang out on the uneven cobbles of the central aisle. 'Howdy, Tom,' he called out, then his leathery face broke into a grin. 'How's the prospecting business?'

'Don't rightly know yet, Jake, I'm still getting meself settled in, so to speak.' He eyed the empty stall and its swept-clean floor which began with a dozen or so rows of neat, even bricks then gave way to rough cobbles. 'Ain't never seen that stall empty afore.'

'Ain't likely to agin, damn fool boy.' He glared at the unhappy youngster. 'Get them bales back in there. I got me a system an' no fool boy's gonna upset it.' He took Tom's arm and steered him away from the stall. 'What in tarnation made you buy out ol' Clem's Weepin' Rock claim. It's played out an' everyone knows it, 'cepting you it seems.' He cocked an enquiring eyebrow.

'Guess I'm an optimist,' Tom parried lightly. 'Seems that since I lost my job I've become a drifter an' drifters ain't too welcome in Prospect, new town rule, so I was told. The only way I could stay around was to get a job, so I bought out Clem's mine an' hired mysel'. Now I'm a working man and own my own property. Ain't a drifter no more.'

'You sure ain't a miner, though.' Jake gave a cackling laugh as he released his grip on Tom's arm, but Tom's smile stayed in place.

'Gotta few minutes to chew the breeze, Jake?'

'Sure, why not.' He turned to the youngster. 'You get an' do what I told you, boy. I'll be back soon an' taking a real good look.' He scowled at the youngster for good measure, then eyed Tom. 'Come on, we'll talk out back.'

'Got me the notion that the gold from the lost patrol is still here somewhere,' Tom said as the two settled arms on the top tail of the corral.

Jake shook his head despairingly and gave him a sad smile.

'You still chasing that old chestnut, son? Give it up. Them hills have been searched by experts ever since the war ended and men have even died trying.' His eyes lifted to the dark mountain range which rose above the rooftops of Prospect, cutting a sawtooth edge against the blue of the sky. 'It ain't a friendly place up there at the best of times. Ain't but one way across them mountains . . . '

'Eagle Pass. You told me that,' Tom interrupted. 'But they never reached the other side where the guns were waiting for them, so where did they go? If'n something happened to them on that trail they or their remains would have been found.'

'Mebbe, mebbe not,' Jake said mysteriously. 'Now why are you so all-fired sure that the gold is still up there?'

'Not up there. Here, in town.'

Jake's eyes widened.

'In Prospect? I ain't following, Tom.'

'Jus' something Ethan Small said afore he died. Now I don't aim for this to be spread about town, but Jed Blake was the Confederate officer who organized the lost patrol. Seems the men were hand-picked for the job, diehard Conferate soldiers loyal to the cause. He settled in Prospect to find out what happened, because he never believed the men he picked would have made off with the gold.'

'What did he believe?' Jake prompted.

'That something happened to the patrol and the gold in Prospect. That mebbe it never left town. That would make sense of the fact that nothing was ever found.'

'The patrol murdered right here in town an' the gold taken?' Jake mused, fingering his chin-whiskers.

'Blake appeared to think so, but somehow, someone found out what Blake was up to, killed him an' his wife and laid the blame on Small. Did you actually see the patrol leave town that night?'

'Not as such,' Jake admitted. 'I wus busy getting the horses bedded down in the stable. The storm I mentioned was coming an' I wanted them in afore it broke, but even so . . . ' Jake shook his head in vigorous denial. 'You're wrong, Tom. Jed Blake was wrong. The wagon was stood outside the livery an' was gone by the time I had got the horses in. Old man Drucker, who owned the livery afore me — I took it over when he died, he said he'd seen 'em leave. Opine plenty o' others had seen the same. Ask around Prospect, reckon you'll hear that they left all right.'

Tom sighed. 'Well, something's going on in this town. Since I spoke up for Ethan Small I've lost my job an' been forced to leave town. I reckon Blake was on to something an' if'n he can find it then I reckon I can too.'

Jake shook his head.

'That's a story that takes a mite o' swallowing. Did Small give any names?'

'No, but there's one man in town who's been real active in blocking every move I make to prove Ethan was innocent of killing the Blakes, an' that's Mayor Tully. Now why do you think that is? Anything to do with the Blakes, Ethan Small or the lost patrol makes the mayor real agitated.'

Jake squinted at him suspiciously.

'Why are you telling me this, Tom?'

'I can't do this on my own, Jake, I need a friend an' they ain't too thick on the ground at the moment.'

'Ain't too sure what you expect me to do, son,' Jake said hesitantly, 'but if'n I can I'll help.'

'Mebbe if'n you tell me what you

meant earlier when you said mebbe, mebbe not when we talked about the gold-wagon disappearing without trace.'

Jake gave a snort and patted the muzzle of a horse who had wandered over.

'If'n they had turned off the trail and entered the 'Snakes' by mistake . . . ' Jake gave a shrug.

'Snakes?' Tom looked puzzled.

'The trail up to Eagle Pass goes through what local folks call 'The Snake-pit', a series of canyons, deep ravines and gullies that run every which way. In daylight the regular trail is easy to follow, but the night the patrol left was dark and stormy. Man could easy mistake the regular trail and make a wrong turn.'

'Even if'n they had, surely something would have been found?' Tom argued.

'The Snakes are something real special. They twist an' turn, sometimes disappear altogether, then come back agin.'

110

Tom stared at the man in amazement.

'How can a canyon disappear then reappear?'

Jake gave a secretive smile.

'You don't know the Snakes, son. When the weather's bad, why them ol' canyons an' such fill up with water. Landslides block off a canyon an' the canyon becomes a lake. Next season the water breaks the landslide down, washes it away an' the canyon comes back. Ain't no one could draw a map of the Snake-pit 'cause it changes so quickly.'

'So you're saying they could be lying at the bottom of a lake.'

'More'n likely buried beneath a rockfall. Sometimes the canyons don't come back. They fill up with rock an' stay that way. The Snake-pit is a bad place. Flash flood, rockfall can strike at any time. If'n you want an answer for why no remains were ever found, I'd stake my money on the Snake-pit being the culprit.'

They spoke for a while longer, then Tom left with his supplies in two small gunny-sacks roped together and hooked over the saddle horn. He returned to Weeping Rock. Apart from the Snake-pit, he had learned nothing new and frustration was beginning to set in. He was getting nowhere. His investigation had virtually ground to a halt before it had really begun. The only place left for him to look was at the Small place, but Emma had made it real clear that he was not welcome. Maybe Ethan had left something that would get him back on the trail.

As he unsaddled his horse he knew he would have to face Emma again, a prospect he did not relish despite Lakota George's assurance that she needed him; it certainly hadn't felt that way on their last meeting. But fate can be a fickle mistress. As he pondered the best way to approach Emma, she instead came to him.

Night tended to come prematurely to Weeping Rock. Outside the canyon the evening sun lay bright over the land. But within, as the sun dipped below the rimrock of the high walls, the canyon filled with a light, hazy shadow. Only the rim of the eastern escarpment caught and held the last vestiges of the sinking sun, painting the high crags gold.

He had just settled his horse in the corral when he heard the chink of metal on stone. He spun, hand dropping to the handle of his holstered pistol, only to find her looking down at him from the back of a roan mare.

'Is that the way you always treat visitors?' she asked coolly, peering down at him from beneath the rim of a tan, low-crowned Stetson.

'The sort o' visitors I'm likely to get, yes,' he replied, relaxing his poised arm.

'Could be too late if they got as close to you as I did before you heard me.'

'The water dripping from the Canyon walls kinda hides other noises.'

She cocked her head and listened. The constant, glasslike tinkling of the dripping water that gave Weeping Rock its name seemed loud in the quiet of approaching night.

'Guess it does,' she said with a nod and looked around. 'I heard you'd taken up prospecting.'

'Just a means to an end,' he replied with a smile. He was more than a little confused at her presence here. She seemed aware of his confusion.

'I came to thank you for what you did for Lakota George in town today.'

'George is a friend, I was just doing what any friend would,' Tom said with a shrug. 'I got coffee on the stove if'n you've a mind to stay a while?' He sounded hopeful.

She smiled. 'I'd like that, Tom,' she said and the way she said his name sent a thrill coursing through him. He stepped forward and gently held the roan's head while she climbed down and stood before him.

'I also came to apologize, Tom. After Pa died I was looking for someone to blame and you walked into it. I had no right to take out my anger and grief on you.' Her voice faltered and she looked away. He released the roan's head and gripped her upper arms.

'There's nothing to apologize for, Emma; after all, I was the man who arrested your pa. I'm just sorry the way it turned out. He saved my life an' I'll be forever beholden to him for that.'

Tears sparkled in her eyes. 'He didn't kill the Blakes, Tom. He couldn't, wouldn't have.'

'I know,' Tom said soothingly, 'but knowing it an' proving it is the big problem. How 'bout that coffee?' He released her arms and she nodded, brushing at the tears on her cheeks.

'Lordy, I must look a sight,' she said self-consciously.

'Never seen a prettier sight,' he responded gallantly.

They drank coffee and talked for almost an hour while the canyon filled up with darkness that never penetrated the cosy confines of the tiny cabin, held at bay by the lambent glow of a kerosene lamp.

Tom told her all that had happened and at last, realizing the lateness of the hour, she made to leave, but turned in the doorway.

'Pa tended to keep notes of things that happened in an old notebook. I can look it out for you.'

'Anything that might help I'd sure appreciate,' he said.

'Why don't you come over for breakfast tomorrow and you can look through it.'

'I'd like that, but reckon I should see you home. It's pretty dark out there.'

'No need, Lakota George is waiting for me at the mouth of the canyon.'

He saw her to her mount and watched her disappear into the darkness, an inner excitement burning within him. More than once he had chided Ethan about his note-taking, a chore the dead man carried out every evening.

'Saves cluttering up my mind with

useless information,' Ethan had replied with a laugh. 'A body cain't remember everything an' as long as it's writ down it ain't gonna be forgot.'

Maybe now the help he needed to prove Ethan's innocence was at hand.

8

Tom was up bright and early the next morning and saddling his horse as the sunlight slid slowly down the western canyon wall. The prospect of one of Emma's breakfasts was something not to be late for. But even as he was up early, there were others who were earlier.

Mayor Tully, along with the banker, Bart Lorimer, and accompanied by Prospect's law in the shape of Nokes and Colson, rode out of town at first light. Tully was eager to complete this particular piece of business as soon as possible. To his mind it would get Tom Morgan out of his hair once and for all and the sooner that was accomplished the better.

It had been the banker who had provided the means when he had disclosed that Ethan Small had died owing the bank $500 on his property. It had been Tully's idea that the bank call in the loan immediately. Get rid of the girl and Morgan would have no need to stay around stirring up trouble; it was as simple as that.

Emma Small had been up early too and felt a happiness that she had not known in a long time as she prepared a table with fresh white linen and got out the best plates. But the happiness was shattered when Lakota George came and told her that four riders were coming in, and who the riders were. Her heart was hammering as she moved out on to the veranda to watch them approach, pausing only briefly to snatch up an old Winchester rifle.

She had it cradled in her arms as the four rode up and came to a halt, line abreast, some ten feet before her. Lakota George had taken up a position midway between the four riders and Emma and now stood, arms folded across his chest staring unblinkingly at the four.

'Morning, Miss Emma, an' it sure has the makings of a mighty fine day to come,' Tully sang out with a smile.

'You're not welcome here, any of you. I'd be obliged if you get off my land,' she called out sharply.

Tully's smile remained.

'That's as maybe to the first part, little lady, but the second part might be a tad questionable. Mind if'n we get down?'

'Yes I do mind. You're not staying.' To give her words force she turned the rifle on the four. It was a gesture on her part; she knew it and, by the looks on their faces, they knew it too.

'You figure on doing a little rabbit-hunting?' Nokes called out.

'I asked you to get off my land,' she said.

Tully shook his head.

'There you go agin with that 'my land' talk. Now that could get you into all kinds of trouble.'

'I don't know what you're talking about,' she said abruptly.

'An' that's why we're here, to put you right afore you go making a fool o' yourself,' Tully said, extracting a cigar from inside his coat. 'Tell her the position, Lorimer.' He snapped out the command whilst making an exaggerated inspection of the cigar.

Bart Lorimer ran a finger around the inside collar of his shirt. He was the least happy of the four.

'It's about the money your pa owed the bank when he died, Miss Small,' he said unhappily.

Emma frowned at him. 'What money?' she demanded.

'It was a bad season last year, it was for everyone. To get him over it he came to the bank and took out a loan.'

'Dammit, Lorimer, we'll be old and grey by the time you get to the point,' Tully cut in harshly. 'To put it in simple words, Miss Small: your pa borrowed five hundred dollars from the bank, well, now the bank's calling in the loan. Can you pay it?'

'I . . . I . . . ' She began.

'Is that a yes or a no?' Tully pressed.

'I've got cattle that will be ready for market soon. When they are sold you'll get your money.'

'Not good enough,' Tully snapped. 'As a major stockholder in the bank, I'm calling in your murdering pa's marker now. Soon ain't good enough.'

'You can't do this,' she protested weakly.

'Tell her, Lorimer.'

'Mayor Tully has the law on his side. Unless you can pay you will have to forfeit this property.'

'In other words, get your pretty little butt outta here,' Mitch Colson called out happily.

She looked at the four and felt tears welling in her eyes. She fought them back.

'I have a thousand head of cattle that are worth a lot more than five hundred dollars. You can take those in payment,' she offered desperately.

Mayor Tully smiled as he lit his cigar. 'That ain't the way we do business, girl. The cattle will, of course, be taken by the bank to pay your debts. Now can you pay the five hundred dollars or not?'

She shook her head.

'You can't do this,' she said dully. 'I can get the money, but it will take a few days.'

'I guess I'll have to take that as a no,' Tully said remorselessly. 'Now that's a pure shame, but we'uns have got to protect them as trust their money to the bank. Sheriff Nokes an' Deputy Colson have been empowered to eject you from this property that is now in the possession o' the bank. Do your duty, boys.' There was a jovial tone in Tully's voice. He enjoyed other people's misery and enjoyed, even more, causing it in the first place.

'Be our pleasure, Mayor,' Nokes called. 'C'mon, Colson.'

'I'd be sure to think twice afore making a move, if'n I was you,' a voice warned. Heads turned to the far corner of the timber-built ranch house as Tom

Morgan kneed his mount forward.

He had seen the arrival of the four and circled around to come in from behind the house. He had heard most of what was said and a cold, dark fury raged within him, but he kept it hidden behind a bland mask.

'Morgan! What in tarnation are you doing here?' Tully cried out.

'Trying to keep you an' your boys from getting shot,' Tom replied.

'An' just who's gonna be doing the shooting?'

'I am if'n them two jokers, who call themselves lawmen, make a move.' Tom's voice hardened and he indicated a double-barrelled shotgun that rested across his left arm, the hand of which held the reins while the fingers of his right hand were curled about the triggers. 'Don't have to be accurate with this thing.'

'Dammit, Morgan you cain't come riding in here threatening folks going 'bout their lawful business,' Tully spluttered out.

'I ain't threatening nobody, jus' pointing out the truth o' the matter. 'Sides I heard tell there was a thousand head o' cattle up for sale an' for jus' five hundred dollars, why that works out at half a dollar each animal; now that's too good to miss. Ain't getting much outta the mine, figure I'll go into the cattle business, recoup my losses so to speak. Can we do business, Miss Small?'

'We can do business, Mr Morgan,' Emma replied, smiling in relief at his appearance.

'That's good, 'cause I have the money on me an' the banker should know; he gave it to me a few days ago.'

Lorimer gave a sickly grin as Tully glared murderously at him.

'You're making a big mistake, Morgan, an' one you'll likely regret,' Tully said sullenly.

'Is that a threat, Mayor?' Tom asked softly, curling an eyebrow.

'Take it how you like,' Tully grated, eyes flashing. 'Nokes, Colson, we're leaving.' He jerked the reins savagely to turn his mount and before departing threw Tom and Emma a last, glaring look. 'You ain't heard the last o' this.'

'Have a nice day, Mayor,' Tom called to the departing three before pulling a roll of notes from his jacket and kneeing his horse forward until he came alongside Lorimer, who was staring after Tully in confusion. 'Here's your money, banker. Now you sign that deed as being fully paid up an' then you can follow your friends.'

Five minutes later Tom watched as Lorimer set his mount to a canter and followed in the direction the others had taken. Emma came forward as Tom dismounted and stood beside him. She slipped an arm through his.

'I should feel happy about this, Tom, but Mayor Tully scares me. I've never seen him like this before.' There was unease in her eyes as she looked up at him.

He smiled at her and wrapped a hand over hers.

'He just doesn't like being made a

fool of. Don't worry 'bout Tully, he'll cool off.' He spoke reassuringly, but deep down he too was worried. Still, his words seem to calm her fears.

'I'll make you out a bill of sale for the cattle,' she said.

'What in tarnation would an old prospector like me want with a herd of cattle? You can pay me back when you sell 'em. Now how 'bout that breakfast you promised. I'm so hungry I could eat a horse.'

She laughed and stood on tip toes to kiss his cheek.

'Thank you, Tom. Let's go eat, you too, George.'

Lakota George's leathery face broke into a grin.

'One thing this ol' Indian has learned is that white man's food is better than Indian.'

As Emma prepared thick bacon slices, eggs and hash browns, Tom looked through the notebooks filled with the late Ethan Small's neat handwriting. Each entry dated, Tom marvelled at the meticulous notes. Ethan wrote about everything that happened even down to the weather conditions of each day.

'Did you find anything in Pa's books, Tom?' Emma asked later as, with breakfast over, she filled cups with dark, aromatic coffee.

'Blake told your pa that he suspected someone in Prospect, but he never named who that suspect might've been, preferring to wait until he had hard evidence. Blake was a cautious man, a little too cautious some might say.'

'Then you've learnt nothing new?' Dismay sounded in her voice.

'Mebbe, mebbe not. Just before he was murdered, according to your pa, Blake was preparing to make a visit to Pine Ridge to see a man called Colonel Ritter. Now it appears this Ritter was the commanding officer at the time the gold shipment was sent out.'

'Did he say why he was going?' Emma asked and Tom shook his head.

'No mention of why that I can find.

Seems that Blake kept that bit o' knowledge to himself.'

Emma's face fell.

'That's it then,' she said dejectedly.

'Mebbe not,' he replied thoughtfully.

'What's on your mind, Tom?'

'That I should make that trip. This Ritter fella may know why Blake was coming to see him. Pine Ridge is only a coupla days ride east of here.'

'Do you think he might?' she asked eagerly.

'It's worth the trip to find out. I'll ride back to the canyon, grab a few things an' head out.' He rose to his feet.

She came forward and wrapped her arms around him, pushing the side of her face against his chest.

'Please be careful, Tom,' she whispered huskily, her voice partially muffled by the fabric of his shirt.

He tilted her face up and kissed her forehead.

'That you can be sure of,' he promised.

She reached up, hands sliding behind

his neck, pulling his face down on to hers in a long, passionate kiss that left them both a little breathless when at last they stepped apart.

'What was that for?' he asked.

'Just to make sure you hurry back,' she replied, red-faced at her own forwardness.

'Yes ma'am.' He touched fingers to his forehead in a mock salute. 'I'll be back before you know it.'

An hour later saw Tom heading east to Pine Ridge, on what could be a wild-goose chase, little knowing that fate was about to hand him a grim surprise.

★ ★ ★

It was in the late afternoon of the fourth day since leaving that Tom, now returning, found himself on the trail approaching Prospect, but long before the town came into sight he had branched off on a smaller trail that would take him to the Small ranch.

It was a perfect evening, the sinking sun sending bars of red through the overhead tree-canopy. He was tired and grimy with trail dust, nothing that a hot tub and a good night's sleep wouldn't cure. Half-asleep, half-awake he was not prepared for the wild figure that leapt from the side of the trail in front of him, waving his arms.

His mount, startled, came to a halt, rising on its hind legs while pawing at the air with its front legs, nostrils flaring and snorting. Tom was almost unseated, but just managed to save himself. His eyes popped in surprise as he brought his mount under control and his jaw dropped. It was not a 'him' but, clad in blue Levis, red-check shirt and hair pushed into a dark Stetson it had been at first an easy mistake to make.

'Emma!' His surprise turned to pleasure at the sight of her and he slid down from his mount. 'That's one heck of a greeting, but you should be more gentle on a saddle-weary fella.' His smile faded at the taut expression on her face and alarm bells sounded. 'What's the matter?'

She rushed forward and gripped his arms.

'Tom, you've got to get out of here, hide before they get you!' There was desperation in her voice.

He shook free of her grip and took her slim shoulders in his hands.

'Emma, you're not making sense,' he said gently.

'It's Mayor Tully, Tom. He was found dead in his office two days ago, his throat had been cut and they're blaming you. Nokes has had a posse out searching for you ever since.'

Tom felt a coldness settle over him at the news.

'Why me?' he asked sharply.

'They found your knife, the one with the Indian's head carved in the handle, on the floor by his body.'

'I ain't seen that knife since the day your pa used it to cut me free. Figured it was lost,' he objected.

'I believe you, Tom, but there's a

whole town up ahead that thinks otherwise. The town council have put out a reward for you. One thousand dollars, dead or alive.'

'An' that's a reward I intend to collect.' Both turned in surprise at the sound of Sheriff Nokes's voice as the man himself stepped from the undergrowth, a Winchester primed and ready for use in his hands. 'Now step aside, girl, an' you, Morgan, get your hands in the air.'

Tom was tensing himself, ready to throw himself at Nokes if the man took a step nearer, but at that moment four others stepped from the undergrowth to join Nokes and surround Tom and Emma.

Slowly, with a sinking feeling, Tom raised his hands.

9

'You finally went too far, Morgan.' A nasty, leering smile dragged at Nokes's lips and his eyes gleamed in anticipation as he stepped closer to Tom.

'You've got it wrong, Nokes. I had nothing to do with Tully's death. Two days ago I was in Pine Ridge. Contact Sheriff Lomax there, he'll confirm my whereabouts. I called in on him.'

'Is that a fact?' Nokes sneered and swung the hard stock of the rifle into Tom's midriff.

Emma screamed and rushed at Nokes, driving small, ineffectual fists into his chest as Tom sank to his knees, winded.

'Someone get this hell-cat off afore I put a bullet in her for aiding a criminal,' Nokes roared and two of the posse leapt forward and grabbed Emma by the arms as Tom came to his feet.

'Don't reckon we need to bother no Pine Ridge lawman about Prospect business,' Nokes sang up, then jabbed out with the rifle again. This time it was aimed at Tom's injured shoulder.

Tom cried out as a wave of agony engulfed his upper chest. He clawed at his shoulder, staggering back against his horse before dropping once more to his knees.

'Leave him alone!' Emma screamed at Nokes. 'He's telling the truth. He went to Pine Ridge four days ago. He was nowhere near Prospect when the mayor was killed.'

Nokes ignored her and nodded at the two remaining possemen.

'Get him to his feet and relieve him of his gun.' As Tom was hauled to his feet, Nokes turned away, leaning his rifle against a tree trunk, and pulling a pair of thin leather gloves from his pocket. He wriggled his hands into them and flexed his fingers in the black leather. Satisfied, he nodded to himself and turned back to Tom who was now in the grip of the two possemen.

'First you side with the Blakes' killer, then you go an' kill the mayor. Reckon we gotta teach you a lesson in right an' wrong afore you get your neck stretched.'

'I had nothing to do with Tully's death,' Tom managed to gasp out before Nokes slammed a fist into his body followed by another and another.

Emma turned her head aside and sobbed as Hoyt Nokes beat Tom brutally about the body and head, splitting his lips and breaking his nose until, at last, Tom sagged into unconsciousness in the grip of the two possemen. By that time Nokes was sweating profusely and his gloves were sticky with the blood that ran freely from Tom's battered face in a gruesome curtain of red that stained his shirt front.

'Get him on his horse. Prospect's gonna have a hanging tomorrow.' He walked across to Emma and turned her head roughly with a blood-soaked hand. 'I ain't finished with you yet, girl, make no mistake. I'll be along to see you directly your boyfriend's swinging by his neck.' Nokes leered down at her before dropping his grip and turning away. 'Mount up, boys,' he called, stripping off the gloves and recovering his rifle. Minutes later Emma was on her own listening to the sound of receding hoof-beats.

She stood in the centre of the trail, hands bunched into small fists at her sides. Tears ran down her cheeks to mingle with Tom's blood smeared on her chin from Nokes's bloody hand. It had become a terrible nightmare of history repeating itself. First her pa accused of a murder he did not commit, now Tom.

She brushed the tears from her eyes and sucked in a big breath. Tom needed help, not tears.

She ran off the trail into the trees to where she had tethered her horse.

★　★　★

Tom groaned and opened his eyes, or rather one eye. The other refused to open, the flesh around it swollen and purple. He lay on his back on something hard and unyielding that did little to help his bruised, aching body. With an effort that tore more groans from his puffy, battered lips he levered himself up on elbows and with a mighty effort, swung his legs down and sat up.

For a minute or two his vision blurred and his head swam, the effort starting up a sickening pounding that throbbed in his temples. He snapped his good eye shut and that seemed to help.

As the pounding subsided to an acceptable dull ache, he opened his eye again. This time his vision remained clear and he was able to take stock of his surroundings. They proved to be very familiar. He was sitting on the hard, wooden bed in the jail in Prospect. Six feet ahead of him the metal bars looked out on to a narrow aisle that gave access to two side-by-side cells. The cells were separated by a set of bars and he could see that the other was unoccupied.

Above the bed, high on the wall behind him, a narrow, barred window allowed a soft glow of light to filter in from the outside. The light had a tinge of red to it; night was coming.

He came gingerly to his feet, the effort starting up other areas of pain that had hitherto remained asleep. Now they protested with sharp stabs. He took a turn around the cell, noting his blood-stained clothes and tenderly probing his battered face with gentle fingers. He could feel the swelling. If it looked as bad as it felt, he was glad he could not see himself.

He worked muscles and joints. It felt as though he had a couple of broken ribs, but no other bones appeared broken.

As the gloom thickened about him a door across the outer aisle opened. Light streamed in, broken up by the form of Mitch Colson. He carried a tray and a grin broke out across his face.

'So you're awake at last, uh? Brung you some grub. Sheriff said we'uns have gotta do things properly. Don't want no prisoners complainin' of ill treatment, even if'n they're gonna hang.'

There was a narrow slot built into the bars at waist-level. Colson passed the tray through and Tom took it.

'Real fine o' the sheriff,' Tom grunted sourly.

'Yep,' Colson agreed and proceeded to light a kerosene lamp hanging from the ceiling outside the cell, continuing to speak as he worked. 'Woulda' come himself, only he hurt his hand subduing a wanted criminal.' Colson chuckled and light flared as he settled the lamp-glass in position and adjusted the wick.

'Send him my condolences,' Tom said flatly as he eyed the tray he held.

It consisted of a plate of meat and potatoes, slice of thick, sourdough bread and a mug of water plus a little addition. Someone had liberally sprinkled it with cigar ash and then dropped the butt of the cigar into the mug of water.

Colson ambled to the bars, grinning. 'What's up, Morgan? Lost your appetite?' He eyed the tray in mock surprise. 'Now how in tarnation did that happen? Reckon I'll have to speak to the chef.' He broke into a giggle that became a harsh, braying laugh. He slapped a thigh with a hand. 'Speak to the chef, I like that one.' He wiped laughter tears from his eyes.

Tom fought back a surge of anger, refusing to react to Colson's cruel joke. He smiled painfully.

'You do that, Mitch,' he mumbled, turned and limped back to the bed. He sat down, the tray on his knees.

Colson frowned. He had expected more of a reaction, and disappointment filled his eyes.

'Is that all you gotta say?' he demanded.

'Perhaps a touch more ash in the

141

gravy,' Tom suggested solemnly.

Colson's frown became a scowl.

'Happen you won't be so damn chirpy when they put that noose around your neck?' He exploded and stamped out of the cell block, slamming the door in his wake.

Left on his own, Tom extracted the cigar-butt from the mug, scraped as much ash as he could from the surface of the water, and after a sniff, drank it. The food he could do without, but his throat cried out for water. The water tasted foul, but it was better than nothing.

Afterwards, setting the tray aside, he lay back. Accused of murder, he had little to look forward to. He knew there would be no trial. What future he had left looked bleak and very short.

Tom spent a restless night. Between troubled dozes he spent long periods listening to the sounds of the night; tinkling piano music filtered in, muffled and muted by the walls; the occasional sound of hoofs; loud, raucous voices as men passed by the front of the jail. At one point, in the early hours of the morning, a couple of gunshots stirred him awake. He thought of Emma Small and the hopes he had built within her, now gone. He fell asleep thinking of her until the first, pale light of dawn greyed the barred window above him.

He sat up as the door leading into the sheriff's office opened and Hoyt Nokes stumbled in. Tom could smell the whiskey on him even before he reached the cell. He carried a mug of coffee, spilling a good part of it on the way. Mitch Colson had followed him, but now lingered in the doorway, grinning foolishly.

'Brung you some coffee.' The mug rattled in the opening. Tom took it, peering at the treacle black contents suspiciously. 'Jus' plain coffee,' Nokes said. 'Figure it only right that a man should be awake for his own hanging.'

'Sure would be a shame if'n he were to fall asleep an' miss it,' Colson called from the doorway and giggled.

'Look, Nokes, whatever you may think o' me, I never killed the mayor. Just send a telegram to Sheriff Lomax in Pine Ridge an' he'll confirm I was with him when the mayor was killed an' then you can start looking for the real killer.'

'Don't need to send no goddam telegram. I got me the real killer an' I'm looking at him right now.' Nokes glared at Tom through the bars. 'You're gonna hang for what you did, Morgan. Up on Tippet's Hill where that old oak stands just as soon as the sun comes up.'

'You go down,' Colson added.

'Don't I even get a trial?' Tom asked bitterly.

'Like the one you gave the mayor?' Nokes laughed. 'Why waste the town's money. We don't need no trial to prove you guilty, we already know you are. Hey, you're a famous man, Morgan. Whole town's gonna be turning out to see you swing. Ain't nothin' worse than an ex-lawman who's gone bad. Ain't that right, Mitch?'

144

'That's right 'nough, Sheriff.' Colson agreed happily.

'Bring 'im out, Sheriff. We'uns have waited long enough!' The demand came from beyond the office. It was followed by a heavy banging at the office door. Nokes eyed Tom.

'Drink your coffee, Morgan. Sounds like folks are getting a mite impatient.'

The banging at the front door became more insistent. It made Tom think of nails being driven into a coffin and he shuddered.

'You gotta wire Sheriff Lomax in . . .'

'I don't gotta do nothin', Morgan. 'Now I reckon it's time, coffee or not. Bring the key, Mitch an' unlock this door.'

Colson grinned and held up a key.

'Already got it, Sheriff.' He strode arrogantly to the cell door and paused uncertainly. He cast Nokes a look. 'What if'n he tries to make a run for it?'

'Then the folks outside'll catch him an' he'll hang sooner. Now get the door open afore them fools outside damage my office.' Nokes stepped away and drew his gun. He suddenly appeared quite sober. 'Try anythin' smart, Morgan, an' I'll put a slug in you. Not enough to kill, but it'll sure slow you down. Slow you down long 'nough to get you to that oak on Tippet's Hill.'

The untouched coffee was taken from him and his hands bound behind his back with a short length of rope. He was then hustled out of the cell, through the office and out into the pre-dawn chill.

Practically the entire town was there, waiting. There were half a dozen or so on horseback, but most were on foot and these surged forward angrily as he appeared. Words like 'killer' and 'murderer' filled his ears.

Nokes stepped forward. On the way through the office he had collected a shotgun. Now he cradled it in his arms.

'You folks step back. The murderer's gonna hang. We're going to the Hill now if'n you folks wanna come along?'

'Wouldn't miss it for anything,' a voice called out. Hate was like a living thing. It washed over Tom in a frightening wave and he felt that, if they could, the crowd would surge forward and tear him limb from limb.

Nokes moved forward and dropped a lariat over Tom's head, pulling it tight to his throat. He grinned evilly at Tom.

'Wouldn't like you to run away now, would we?' He climbed into the saddle of his horse and after twisting the end of the rope about the saddle horn, kneed his mount forward. On shaking, unwilling legs, Tom was forced to follow while the crowd jeered.

There were some on the sidewalks who disagreed with what was happening, but they were in the minority. They could only watch, tight-lipped and grim-faced. One such was Seth Haggerman.

Tom turned desperate eyes on him.

'I was in Pine Ridge with Sheriff Lomax when Tully was killed,' he yelled hoarsely, hopelessly, even though he knew that he was beyond help now.

A stone hit Tom in the back, but the pain from that was overshadowed by the fear of what was to come. If a hanging was done right, it broke the neck and death was swift. If it was done wrong a man suffocated to death and that was not quick. A shiver went through Tom. He stumbled on ever-weakening legs and refused to give in to the fear.

A second stone caught him on the side of the head next to his right eye and blood began to flow. The crowd found this amusing and stones began to rain in on Tom. It was Nokes who eventually put a stop to it.

'Quit that,' he yelled. 'You're gonna injure my damn horse.'

Up on the hill, the lone oak-tree that had been there since before the town was built, waited. Over one thick limb a noose hung ready.

Tom's mouth was dry and his heart was like a caged bird trying to escape. He felt sure that at any second now his heart would burst through his ribs.

A single rider waited by the oak. The rider was clad in a long, black duster buttoned to the neck. A high domed hat sat upon his head, brim pulled down shielding the rider's face. The hands holding the reins were clad in black, leather gloves.

Tom shivered. The hangman would be Mace Grindle. He was the official hangman for the county. He lived just outside Prospect, spending much of his time travelling from town to town carrying out his grim business.

'We wus lucky to find ol' Mace at home,' Nokes called back conversationally. 'He's got a hanging down Pecos way at the end o' the week.' Nokes grinned back at Tom. 'You sure are looking a mite peaky, boy.'

'Nuthin' a good hanging won't cure,' Mitch Colson sang back and both men laughed.

They reached the oak and Nokes climbed from the saddle as the crowd gathered in a circle.

'Reckon you can use my cayuse, boy,' he said genially as he took the rope from Tom's neck and coiled it. 'Some o' you men. Get him in the saddle.'

There was no lack of helpers and Tom found himself in the saddle, facing east, the sun already beginning to show behind the sharp peaks of the Sierra Diablo Mountains.

'He's all yours, Mace. Swing him high,' Nokes called out. The black-garbed rider nodded, kneed his mount alongside Tom and placed the noose over Tom's head. 'Gotta do it proper like. Wait until the sun clears the ridge.'

The chatter from the crowd had died down now as every head craned to the east to watch the rising sun.

Sweat stood out on Tom's face

'I didn't do it!' he croaked out. 'You hang me an' the real killer of the mayor will go free.'

'We done got the real killer, Morgan, sitting on a horse with a rope around his neck,' Colson called back.

There was a sudden sigh from the

crowd as the sun lifted clear of the mountains and balanced itself delicately on the high ridges, sending a golden glow sweeping across the land.

'Time to go, Morgan.' Nokes moved to the rear end of the horse Tom sat astride and lifted his hand, still holding the coiled lariat, ready to strike the horse's rump and send it galloping forward.

Tom closed his eyes as he waited for oblivion.

10

Instead of the horse bolting from beneath him to leave him hanging and choking at the end of a rope, a terrific explosion rent the air. Tom snapped his eyes open in time to see the front of the bank explode outwards in a ball of flame and smoke that surged the width of Main Street. It was followed by a second explosion that destroyed the sheriff's office.

The few people who hadn't joined the hanging party were now running about Main Street in obvious panic as a third explosion, from behind the saloon, sent a cloud of smoke and flame lifting high into the air.

'My bank!' Bart Lorimer wailed, eyes wide. He began pushing his way through the crowd, which was already breaking up as, the lynching forgotten, people began running back into the town. Flames were licking hungrily at the front of the bank and the sheriff's office, and as the town was made mostly of wood, fire was to be feared. If it took a hold the whole town could be wiped out.

'What the hell's going on?' Colson cried out.

'That's my damn office!' Nokes roared.

Temporarily forgotten in the confusion, Tom could only stare in awe at the sudden and unexpected destruction. But then something else happened that made him forget that.

The noose was lifted from his neck and the rope binding his wrists slashed through, freeing him. Hoyt Nokes caught the flash of silver out of the corner of his eye and snapped his head around in time to see Mace Grindly cut Tom's bonds and astonishment flared in his eyes.

'Dammit, Mace. What are you doing?' His mind was still reeling with the strange attack on the town. Now, with the hangman cutting the prisoner loose, it was almost too much for his dazed mind to take in. He began to claw his gun free from its holster as the hangman slapped the rump of Tom's horse and the animal, unnerved by the earlier explosions, surged forward. Tom barely had time to retrieve the hanging reins before the animal, ears laid back, broke into a gallop.

The hangman set his horse in motion, steering it in Nokes's general direction, then veering away. At the same time he lifted a foot from the stirrup and drove the heel into Nokes's face. With a yell of pain Nokes went sprawling into a thorn thicket.

Mitch Colson turned at the sound of the sheriff's cry in time to see a horse bearing down on him. He tried to throw himself out of the way, but the animal's hard-muscled shoulder caught him in the back and sent him sprawling heavily to the ground.

Hunched low over the horse's neck, Tom dug his heels in. Behind him he heard galloping hoofs. He snapped a quick look over his shoulder to see the dark-clad hangman following him. He knew Mace Grindly. A dour, taciturn man who kept himself to himself. It was totally out of character for him to have done what he had. Mace enjoyed his job too much. In fact, for what he had done he would probably end up on the end of another hangman's rope. It just didn't make sense. On the other hand, who cared about sense? He was free.

The black-garbed rider drew level with Tom as they entered a copse of trees. As yet they were not being followed, the townsfolk of Prospect too concerned with saving their town to worry about an escaped 'murderer' and a deranged hangman.

The rider took the lead and indicated a narrow trail to the right which led into a maze of gullies and ravines that rippled the land like blankets on an unmade bed. It was not long before the land had swallowed them up. Tom temporarily lost his saviour ahead, but as the narrow gully opened into a wide, dried-up riverbed, the rider was waiting for him.

Tom brought his mount to a halt with only a few yards separating them. The rider's head was tilted down, the brim of the hat hiding his face.

'I'm obliged for what you did, but I ain't sure why you did it,' Tom began, then his mouth fell open as the rider lifted his head and removed the hat, freeing a cascade of chestnut curls.

'Because I love you, Tom Morgan an' I don't intend to lose you without a fight.' Emma Small smiled brightly across at Tom and had to laugh at the dumbstruck expression that filled Tom's face. 'Sometimes a woman's gotta be as tough as a man if'n she's to get on out here.' She kneed her mount forward until the two were side by side and concern swept the amusement from her eyes. She pulled her gloves off and touched his battered face with gentle fingers. 'Your poor face,' she murmured.

Her touch felt like the soft wings of a butterfly. He caught the hand and kissed the fingers.

'Huh. Indian kiss more than fingers of girl who saved his life.' A dry, welcome voice called out and Tom sat up guiltily, dropping her hand as Lakota George appeared, leading two horses.

Tom eyed the Indian in amazement.

'You were the one who blew up half the town.'

'Only a little bit,' George corrected. 'Miss Emma said to cause a diversion.'

'You did that all right,' Tom said with a laugh as he slid from his horse. Emma also dismounted, taking off the black duster to reveal her range clothes beneath. 'Did Mace Grindly object to your taking his clothes?' Tom raised an enquiring eyebrow.

'He was a tad obstructive at first, but George can be very persuasive.' She cast an eye on the old Indian and he smiled. 'We left him tied up in his cabin. Someone should find him soon.'

'That was some risk you took, up there on the hill. If'n they'd'a caught you it would probably have been a double hanging,' Tom said seriously.

'Mebbe,' she said. 'But all anyone sees of Mace is his black hat and coat. When we found out that you were going to hang at dawn, we knew that Mace Grindly's services would be called on.' She grimaced at the thought. 'Knowing that he likes to get everything set up beforehand, it wasn't difficult to take his place and be there waiting for when they brought you out. All eyes would be on you and not me. Once George set the dynamite off . . . ' she shrugged. 'Well, you know the rest.'

'What in tarnation did I do to deserve friends like you?' Tom gazed in admiration at the two.

'You ain't gonna kiss my hand, are you?' Lakota George asked suspiciously and both Tom and Emma laughed. For Tom, it felt good to laugh. It was something he had not been able to do for a while. 'I brought your horse and got your gunbelt from the sheriff's office, before it fell down,' George said with a dead-pan face.

Tom buckled the gunbelt on. 'Things sure are getting better as the day goes on,' he said.

'But it won't stay that way,' Emma pointed out. 'Once the town is safe they'll come looking for you, for us. We've got to get away from here. Perhaps ride north or head for Mexico.'

Tom held up a hand.

'I'm obliged you saved my neck, but I ain't leaving here until I find out who killed the mayor an' laid the blame on me. And I hope it'll lead to who killed the Blakes and clear your pa's name.'

Emma's eager look faded.

'Tom, they'll kill you if they find you.'

He stalked forward and laid his hands on her shoulders.

'I can't run, Emma. If'n I do, I'll spend the rest of my life looking over my shoulder, never knowing peace. Never knowing who's gonna be around the next corner.'

Tears dampened her eyes and she lowered her head. 'I don't want you to die, Tom,' she said in a small voice.

He lifted her head.

'I don't intend to. Lakota George can take you somewhere safe and I'll join you when everything's settled here.'

She drew away from him, hostility flaring in her eyes.

'I didn't save your hide, Tom Morgan, for you to go getting it full of holes. If you stay, I'll stay.' She placed her hands on her hips and glared defiantly at him.

Tom glanced across at Lakota George. The Indian crossed his arms over his chest.

'I stay too.'

Tom looked from one to the other helplessly, then shrugged.

'Let's go catch ourselves a killer then,' he said.

Hoyt Nokes, looking a little the worse for wear, scratches on his hands and face from his encounter with the thorn-bush, nose swollen, had taken up temporary quarters in the saloon. He had commandeered Chuck Clayton's back room to use as an office. It was midday, the fires had been put out, order restored and now the saloon was full. Nokes had called a meeting. He stood with his back to the bar facing a sea of faces.

'Ain't no doubt 'bout it,' he started out as soon as the saloon had quietened down. 'It was that Small girl and the goddam Injun who set Morgan free. They tied ol' Mace up, took his clothes an' while she dressed up, the Injun dynamited the town.' A rumble went through the crowd at his words. 'I'm heading up a posse to catch these varmints an' I'm looking for volunteers.' He swept a fierce gaze around the saloon. A gaze that opened up into a smug smile as nearly every man raised a hand. He gave a satisfied nod.

'What we gonna do when we find 'em?' a voice called out.

'Well we ain't gonna dance with 'em

an' that's for sure,' Nokes called back and a laugh went up from the crowd. He raised his hands for quiet. 'If'n you can't bring 'em in alive then dead's the next best thing. The banker here, Mr Lorimer, has put up a reward of a thousand dollars a head for each of 'em, dead or alive. So that should give you boys more'n a passing interest in getting 'em.' A ragged cheer went up from the crowd.

'What if'n they've already lit out, Sheriff. Could be well outta the county by now?' someone asked.

'Getting me some wanted flyers printed up an' they'll be sent to all the towns around. They won't git far. Man, woman an' Injun travelling together, soon be spotted. In the meantime, we got some searching to do. Could be they's hiding out nearby. Reckon we got 'nough men for four posses, that way we can cover each direction at the same time. Milt, Curly, you head two posses, one go east, the other west. Rest of you men come with me and

Colson. I'll take north, Mitch here, south. Any questions?'

'Do we kill the woman? I ain't too sure I can do that?'

'Mister, if'n she's shooting at you, remember, her bullets can kill just as much as those fired by a man. I reckon then you'll be shooting to kill. If'n you do catch her alive, bring her to me.' He fingered his swollen nose. 'Got me some unfinished business with that bitch.'

His words brought a general peal of coarse laughter and even coarser suggestions from the assembled men.

'Gents!' Chuck Clayton appeared behind the bar. 'Those doing posse work, step up to the bar for a free drink.'

There was a stampede to the bar following his words.

*   *   *

The three had watched as the four posse groups rode out of town. Tom

163

was impressed that Nokes could organize such a large attendance.

'Guess we riled 'em up some,' he commented drily.

'Indian diversion,' Lakota George replied.

It was easy to evade the searchers in the foothills of the Guadalopes. By nightfall, as the weary and less than enthusiastic posse groups returned to town, Tom, Emma and Lakota George were camped on a pine-crowned bluff, ten miles to the north-west of Prospect. During the late afternoon they had seen a cloud of smoke rising to the east of their position and it wasn't hard to pinpoint the area as being where Emma's ranch house lay. There were tears in Emma's eyes as she looked at the column of smoke.

'Guess they fired your home. I'm sorry, Emma,' Tom said contritely.

She brushed away the tears and forced a smile. 'It's not your fault, Tom.' She laid a hand on his arm. He could feel her trembling through the touch. 'Besides, it stopped being a home when Pa died.'

He took her in his arms and held her tight.

'I'll make it up to you,' he promised.

As the purple shadows of dusk began to flow over the land, Lakota George scraped out a hollow behind a thicket of scrub and lit a small fire. The two had brought some grub along, but it would not last long. Over what was, for Tom, a very welcome cup of coffee, they discussed what their next move should be.

'Like as not, Nokes will have men out agin tomorrow, searching the area,' Tom brooded. The glow from the embers of the fire reddened his face.

'So, we avoided them today, we can do the same again tomorrow,' Emma said.

'But we can't go on running for ever,' Tom pointed out. 'Why was Tully killed? If'n we can figure out that then mebbe we can work out who the killer is most likely to be.' He eyed the ember-lit faces of the other two.

Lakota George returned his glance.

'Don't ask me, I'm just a dumb Indian.'

Tom smiled at the other's droll reply, but his mind was elsewhere.

'It all comes back to the lost patrol an' the gold they were carrying. We know from your pa's notes that Blake came here to investigate the missing gold and also that he hit on some clue in town.'

'Something that he was going to see that colonel in Pine Ridge about, but he was killed and Pa accused before he could make that journey.' Emma took over the thought process from Tom.

'Colonel Ritter.' Tom nodded. 'It was an ol' tintype taken of the patrol standing by the wagon.'

'Well, that's it,' Emma said excitedly. 'If, as you suspect, the wagon never left Prospect that night, maybe some of the men from that patrol are now residents of Prospect and the picture would identify them?'

Tom shook his head. 'I hear what you're saying, Emma, but I've seen that tintype. Ain't a man on it that I recognize. I've got the tintype in my saddle-bag. You're welcome to take a look at it tomorrow when the light is better, but I reckon you'll come to the same conclusion as me.'

'Oh!' Her face fell.

'OK. Let's look at it from a different angle. What if'n a few of Prospect's citizens at the time decided to take the gold for themselves. The war was nearly over. The Union soldiers were marching through all the Southern states. Mebbe someone decided that the gold shouldn't go any further, figuring that it would probably end up in Union hands anyway. So they killed the patrol and hid the gold.'

'Why hide the gold? Maybe they just took off and kept going,' Emma questioned.

'If'n that had happened, citizens gone missing, the army would have been on to it straight away. No, for what it's worth, I think it's still in Prospect. Mebbe they, whoever they are, take a little at a time. Melt it down? Change its shape?' Tom shrugged. 'The only way I'm gonna find out for sure is to get this murder charge agin me dropped an' then I'll have more time to find out the truth.'

'How are you gonna do that?' Emma asked.

'Sheriff Lomax in Pine Ridge can vouch for my whereabouts on the day Tully was killed. I'll need to get a message to him.'

'Why don't we all ride to Pine Ridge?' Emma asked, eyes darting from one to the other.

'Nokes is gonna have every trail outta the county covered. No, it's gotta be someone they'd never suspect.' He dropped into a thoughtful silence, then snapped his fingers. 'Jake Bundy. He'll do it. He does a stage run to Pine Ridge every other week. He's backed me up so far. I have to go an' see him.'

'Go back to Prospect?' Emma's eyes

popped. 'Tom, you can't, it'll be madness.'

'I know the back ways into Prospect better'n most. I can slip into town under cover of darkness. Jake's a late bird. He's still up and about when the town's asleep. I'll go tomorrow night.' He nodded to himself.

'It'll be dangerous, Tom,' Emma objected. 'You'll be caught for sure.'

'That's what it is now an' it ain't gonna get better,' Tom pointed out. 'We can dodge the posses for a few days, but sooner or later we'll be seen. No, this is the best way. It's the only way.'

'I hope you're right,' Emma said, but there was a doubtful tone in her voice.

'You don't want diversion, Indian style, then?' Lakota George spoke up for the first time.

'Hell no,' Tom said with a laugh. 'I think I want the rest of the town to remain standing.'

11

Darkness had long since fallen the following night when Tom, leaving his horse in a stand of trees, made his way through the back lots on the western side of Prospect. It was close to midnight, but the piano-player was still working hard in the saloon. It was a moonless night and for that Tom was grateful.

During the day they had moved further into the foothills where the ravines cut deeper and bluffs rose higher. From a high vantage point they had watched distant riders pass by. Emma had examined the tintype and had to confess that none of the eight men shown there resembled a younger version of anyone in Prospect today.

'Well, Mr Blake must have had some reason for wanting the tintype,' she had declared, frustration charging her voice.

'Whatever it was died with him,' he had replied.

A few cabins showed light as he slipped past them, but most were in darkness. Voices followed by sudden spasms of coarse laughter floated out from Main Street, mingling with the jangling piano and occasional feminine squeals of delight. Even at this time of night riders appeared on Main Street and once a wagon lumbered through, metal-shod wheels crunching, harness jingling. It seemed far busier and noisier than he remembered, but in those days he hadn't been creeping about trying not to be seen.

The journey to the livery stable took a little over ten minutes from where he had tied his mount, but it seemed a lot longer.

Jake Bundy was sitting out front of his little cabin behind the livery stable when Tom arrived. The old man was supping whiskey. A lamp hanging from a beam of the overhang cast a soft, yellow glow over him. Nearby a horse whickered as it sensed Tom passing by. It moved away nervously, metal shoes clinking on stone.

As Tom reached the edge of a small barn, a dry twig snapped under his feet. The effect on Jake was instantaneous. The whiskey glass was banged down on the table next to him and he grabbed up a shotgun leaning against the wall. The dry clicking of the hammer being pulled back fell heavy on Tom's ears.

Jake came out of his chair.

'Come out, you varmint. I kin hear you skulking 'bout in the dark. Don' need to aim this gun, jus' pull the trigger an' you'll be picking buckshot outta your hide till Thanksgiving.'

Tom stepped clear of the barn. 'Ease up on the trigger finger, Jake. It's me, Tom Morgan.'

'Tom? Step out so's I kin see you.' Tom did as he was bid, moving forward into the light. 'Dammit, Tom. What the hell you doing? Creeping 'bout in the darkness trying to give an' old man a heart attack. Coulda' got yoursel' killed.' Jake put the rifle aside.

'If'n I'd come in daylight I woulda' been,' Tom replied.

Jake pumped Tom's hand in greeting.

'What in tarnation are you doing here, boy?' Jake demanded. 'Figured you'd ha' been clean outta the county by now.' He gave a chuckle. 'That sure was something at the hanging though. They said that it was that girl, Emma Small, that took ol' Mace's place while the Injun rearranged the town wi' some blow-sticks.'

'I had me some help,' Tom admitted.

'Ol' Mace, he's fit to bust.' Jake chuckled again. 'Here, boy, take a seat. Whiskey?'

'Nothin' for me, Jake, but I could do with a little help.'

'If'n there's anything I kin do that don't put me at the end of a hangman's noose, I'll do it, Tom. Never did hold with the idea that you killed the mayor.'

'Sheriff Lomax in Pine Ridge can vouch for where I was when the mayor was killed. I need you to get a message

173

to him. I know you do a run to Pine Ridge.'

Jake nodded his head.

'Going to Pine Ridge day after tomorrow. Knows me the sheriff too. Reckon I kin do that.'

Tom breathed a sigh of relief and pulled a square of folded paper from his pocket.

'Be obliged if'n you could, Jake. It's all written down here. If'n you could give it to him it'd get me out of a whole heap o' trouble.' He passed to Jake the note he had written during the day.

Jake took it.

'I'll do that for sure, Tom,' he promised. 'Where you folks at? I'll need to contact you after I've been to Pine Ridge.'

'We're not at any one place. Gotta keep moving.'

'You need somewhere safe to rest up while I'm gone,' Jake said. 'Get caught for certain ridin' around. Feeling's real bad in town, Tom. They'll string you an' the Injun up on sight. The girl . . . ' He looked decidedly uncomfortable. 'Truth is, they got other plans for her afore they hang her. You need a safe place, for her sake.'

Tom felt a chill spread through him at Jake's words.

'I know what you're saying, Jake, but there ain't no place safe,' he said unhappily.

'There might be one such place. The little lady needn't worry 'bout the likes of Nokes or Colson, but it's as dangerous as hell and the one place no one will come looking.' Jake eyed Tom keenly.

'Figure you're talking 'bout the Snakes?' Tom said slowly.

'Yep,' Jake replied. 'Ain't a place that's friendly to man. Kill a man in the blink of an eye, but . . . ' He shrugged. 'I kin take you folks to where I know, but then it's up to you. I'll be away three, mebbe four days. That's a long time to be dodging posses an' you'll be safe in the Snakes 'til I get back.'

Tom nodded. 'Sounds good.'

Jake smiled. 'I'll meet you folks at Eagle Pass, sundown tomorrow.'

'What if'n you're seen?'

'I'm out doing a little private tracking on my own. The banker's put up a thousand dollars a head, dead or alive, on each of you, an' I don't wanna split the reward with a lot o' other rannies.'

'I didn't know,' Tom said, shocked.

'There are a few loners out there already an' when Nokes gets his flyers printed an' posted, they'll be a lot more. Prospect'll become a bounty hunter's paradise.'

Tom nodded. 'Thanks for the warning, Jake. 'Preciate it.'

'Be waiting for me at sundown. Now what about that whiskey?'

'I'll drink a bottle of it with you when this is all over, but until then . . . sundown, tomorrow.' Tom vanished into the darkness a few minutes later. The news about the reward had badly shaken him. Coupled with Nokes's flyers, time was running out fast. He needed to get back to the others to give them the unwelcome news.

Jake was true to his word. Hidden in a clump of box elder they watched him ride to the mouth of the pass and pause; he had a pack-mule in tow with a couple of gunny-sacks strapped to its back. He nodded briefly at them and then led them into the pass. Tom wondered what the mule was for, but as Jake said nothing he did not press the point.

It was a journey that led them up through the heart of the mountains. Up through high-walled canyons, away from the prairie. Sycamore and elm gave way to pine and cedar the higher they climbed. An hour later they reached the 'Snake-pit'. The red ball of the sun had already begun its slide behind the western rimrock and the shadows of approaching night gathered darkly around them.

Here the weather had eroded the rocks, worn them away until they looked like a mouthful of rotten, decaying teeth encircling a grey plateau.

The plateau was split and seamed with cracks and crevices that gave way to ravines and canyons, lined with banks of sloping scree. They were faced with a bewildering number of crumbling canyon mouths to enter.

'I see what you mean about it being a mite confusing up here,' Tom said, kneeing his mount alongside Jake.

'In a storm, like it was on the night the lost patrol vanished, a man could easy take the wrong way,' Jake said seriously. He pointed to a canyon to the right of the one that lay straight ahead. 'That's the one they shoulda taken an' they'da been safe.'

'Where are we headed?' Tom wanted to know.

Jake nodded to the left.

'That's the way, boy. Leads down through a cavern into a whole mess of caves and tunnels. Here.' He passed the reins of the pack-mule to a surprised Tom. 'Put me some grub together for you folks, some feed for the horses and there's a coupla oil-lamps, tends to be black as night down there. You'll find water in some o' the caves. Should be 'nough supplies there to last four, five days. I'll be back in at noon, four days from now, five at the latest. Good luck to you, folks. Hey, you might even find the lost patrol and its gold.' He cackled as he wheeled his horse.

''Preciate the food an' such, Jake,' Tom said.

'Figured you wouldn't have much with you.'

'I'll pay you back when this is all over,' Tom promised.

'Ain't no need. You folks take care now.'

'Thanks for what you are doing for us, Mr Bundy,' Emma called.

'Tain't nothin', ma'am. Just pleasured you came to me fer help and glad that I was able to give it. Now you take care. The Snakes ain't gotta liking for man or woman and I reckon we might be due some rain soon.' He nodded towards some distant peaks where whirls of dark cloud were gathering and spreading out across the blue sky.

They watched Jake move off.

'Let's go check out our new home,' Tom said cheerfully. He kneed his horse in the direction of the indicated canyon.

The canyon shelved steeply down. It was littered with loose scree and the horses' hoofs slipped continually. Above them the sky became a thin, blue line as they dropped ever deeper. Eventually the ground levelled out and the mouth of a cave beckoned them.

Tom dismounted, rooted out a lamp from the pack-mule. At the cave mouth he lit the lamp with a lucifer.

'Reckon it'll be better if'n we lead the horses,' he called to the other two.

The cave mouth opened into a large cavern, the roof too high for the lamplight to reach. The sound of the horses' hoofs clip-clopped back and forth with an eerie echo. They entered a tunnel, its dark walls slick with damp. Water dripped from the roof to add to their discomfort, the icy droplets soaking into their clothes.

Passing into a small cave they splashed through ankle-deep, icy water, the cloying darkness wrapping itself around them like a dark shroud.

'How much further, Tom?' Emma called out after a bit.

'Soon, Emma. Reckon to find a cave that ain't too wet where we can stop.'

'Caves are for bears and bats,' Lakota George spoke up.

'And people who go around blowing up towns,' Tom riposted, trying to maintain a lightness of spirit that he did not feel. He heard Emma giggle and that made him feel better.

'There's light up ahead,' he called out excitedly some ten minutes later as a murky greyness lit a tunnel-opening ahead. A few minutes later they entered a high, wide cavern. One side was breached by a roughly square opening, perhaps eight feet high and as much wide. They moved to the opening and peered cautiously out.

Emma reeled back with a gasp. In the last remaining minutes of fading daylight left they glimpsed a chasm that dropped sheer to an unseen bottom far, far below. The opening looked across to another sheer, grey wall some fifty feet away. It was like looking out of a window from the top of an impossibly high building. They backed away from it and turned their attention to the cavern. Apart from being big it was dry and towards the back a pool of cold, clear water offered them the chance to slake their thirsts.

'Well, I reckon this is home for the next few days. But watch out for the front door, it's got one hellava step down.' Tom grinned boyishly at his own joke.

There were three openings in the wall at the rear of the cavern and one in the wall at the far side, opposite the one by which they had entered. After a cursory examination of each they settled down to see what Jake had brought them. It turned out to be jerky, sourdough bread and a block of cheese. None too exciting, but enough to keep hunger at bay. He had also added some blankets.

A coffee-pot and some coffee had been included and Tom was ready to jump for joy until he realized they had nothing with which to make a fire to boil the pot on. It was Lakota George who provided a solution.

He found a section of bone-white tree-limb wedged in one corner. It was dry and enough to provide a small fire for one evening. The Indian broke it up and soon had a fire going. Later the delicious aroma of hot coffee filled the air.

'Probably washed in here during a flash flood at one time,' Tom surmised after they had fed and settled back with full mugs of coffee.

Lakota George had built the fire near to the chasm-opening in order to let any smoke escape. Night had taken over outside and unseen clouds had spread darkly across the sky, blotting out the stars. As they sat there they heard the first rumblings of distant thunder.

Emma shivered.

'Let's hope we don't get any flash floods,' she opined.

The thunder became more persistent as night drew near and darkness filled the chasm. Tom had lit a lamp, and sitting by it, he studied the tintype.

'There's gotta be something here that we are not seeing,' he said after a while. 'Eight men and a wagon.' He tossed the tintype aside and rubbed weary eyes.

'You look tired, Tom,' Emma said. She sat next to him, a blanket over her knees, their backs leaning against a boulder. Lakota George sat opposite, cross-legged on his blanket. The lamp sat on the floor between them.

'You ever been married, George,' Tom asked, dragging his mind from the tintype.

'Have known many fine maidens. Lakota maiden fine woman.' The Indian nodded. 'Miss Emma, she make fine Lakota maiden. Make Indian brave howl at the moon.'

Emma looked up in surprise, a blush

stealing across her face.

'George, that's enough,' she admonished, but there was a hint of laughter in her voice.

'I think you're right there,' Tom agreed with a laugh.

'If I was five summers younger . . . '

'Make that fifty,' Tom, responded.

'Boys, will you stop it,' Emma pleaded, but secretly enjoying the word-play between the two.

A rumble of thunder, the loudest they had heard, shook the cavern. Dust floated down from the roof. The horses whickered in panic and pawed the floor, hoofs ringing out their unease. Lakota George went across to them and Emma snuggled against Tom as lightning lit up the chasm outside.

'I don't think I'm gonna get much sleep tonight,' she said as thunder exploded through the cavern again and outside the rain began to fall.

Unable to sleep, Tom had returned to studying the tintype. Lakota George was still tending the horses while

Emma had fallen asleep on his shoulder.

He frowned in concentration as Lakota George sang an Indian song to the troubled beasts. His eyes flicked from men to wagon, wagon to men. Thunder pounded at the mountain, lightning flared in brief, dazzling spurts. Tom was about to lay the tintype aside when something caught his eye. He stared at the tintype, feeling a cold wash of horror sweep over him. It was there, it had been all along. He knew why Blake had wanted the tintype.

'Oh, Jesus, no!' The words flew from his lips.

Emma stirred at his side and sat up, rubbing her eyes. She looked at Tom's stricken face with concern.

'What's the matter, Tom?'

He looked at her.

'I've been a fool, Emma, and I may have cost us all our lives.'

'Tom, you're not making sense.' There was a note of alarm in her voice.

He waved the tintype.

'It's not the men, it's the wagon.' Thoughts were running chaotically through his mind. 'No, not the wagon, but the wheels.' By now Lakota George had come across, hearing the alarm in Emma's voice.

'Tom, you're still not making sense,' Emma pleaded.

'Why in tarnation didn't I see it afore. Look at the wheels. They're double spoked around the hub. I remember Colonel Ritter saying it was to give the wheels extra strength for carrying the gold.'

Emma shrugged. 'So it's a little different,' she agreed. 'But not unusual.'

'No, that's where you are wrong, and if'n I'm right, it'll take us straight to the killer. I've seen this double-spoke arrangement afore. It's in Prospect, there for all to see. I've seen it time and time agin until it just becomes part of the town and in the end you don't take any notice of it.'

'Where have you seen it?' Emma prompted.

Tom gave a bitter laugh and shook his head in resignation.

'It hangs over the doors of the livery stable. Blake was right, the gold never left Prospect.' His mind remembered something else he had seen. 'And I've a good idea where it is.'

'I'm not sure I know what you're saying, Tom,' Emma said hesitantly.

'I'm saying that the fellas in that tintype were murdered and the gold taken by their own Confederate kind. And that Jake Bundy was one of their murderers.' He shook his head and snorted. 'It makes sense of why nothing was ever found of the wagon. What better place to hide it than in a livery stable amongst all the other wagons and parts of wagons? I wouldn't be surprised if'n the bodies o' the murdered men weren't buried under the stable.'

'But Jake, the same Jake who helped us?' Emma said helplessly.

'He didn't help us, he helped himself. He's buried us in a mountain that he

188

knows is unstable. He wants us out of the way as much as Tully did, but I guess Tully's methods were creating too much public interest, so eventually he had to get rid o' him. He must have found my knife, that I thought was lost at the river, and used it to kill Tully. Jake an' Tully were partners who fell out in the end, an' I guess there are others. I reckon Jake an' the gold are going to be leaving Prospect pretty soon and unless we get outta here pretty quick, he's gonna get away with it.' Tom climbed to his feet.

'It's so hard to believe,' Emma protested faintly.

'Two men, two different ways of dealing with things. Tully was the bully, Jake, the amiable old uncle-figure. He sent us down here for a reason an' I ain't got a good feeling 'bout it.'

'Tom, stop, you're scaring me,' Emma protested.

'We've got to get out o' here now, afore it's too late.' Tom's eyes flickered around nervously as an extra loud peal of thunder rocked the cavern, making the hairs on the back of Tom's neck bristle. It sounded different from the others. To his ears it sounded like dynamite going off! As the sound faded away another took its place. A low, hissing rumble. It seemed to be coming from the rear of the cavern and was growing louder.

Emma came to her feet, clutching at Tom's arm.

'What is it, Tom?'

The answer came a few seconds later as from the three tunnels at the rear of the cavern there burst three jets of foaming water which joined together in a single wall of water, racing towards them, exploding over the boulders in great fans of dancing white spray.

The horses whinnied in terror, their cries awful to be heard, as the wall of water overwhelmed them. Tom grabbed up the lamp and took hold of Emma's hand.

From the tunnel mouth to the left a torrent of water burst into the cavern.

'Run!' Tom hollered, indicating to Lakota George the tunnel by which they had entered as the first surge of water swirled around their ankles, threatening to pull their feet out from under them.

'The horses!' Lakota George called out. He began struggling against the rising flow of water towards them.

'George, no! It's too late,' Tom yelled above the rumble and hiss of the water. If the Indian heard, he paid no attention, forcing himself forward in the now waist-high torrent.

'George!' Emma screamed.

Beyond the cavern, lightning danced above the chasm, illuminating the thick white arc of water erupting through the opening in the wall before it plunged into the chasm.

The terrified horses twisted and turned in the rushing, foaming water, then one fell, crashing into another and then another, to be swept away to the awful drop into the chasm.

In the dim, uncertain light of the

lamp which Tom was still holding up, Lakota George saw leg-thrashing horses sweep past him on either side. He didn't see the pack-mule until it hit him and by then it was too late.

In mounting horror, Tom saw the Indian go down. Emma screamed as man and animals, now in a hopeless tangle, were swept from the cavern to their deaths.

Still holding on to the lamp, an arm now around Emma's waist, Tom fought the flow as he dragged himself and Emma towards the tunnel. Water from the cavern was pouring into it, but it was their only hope of salvation. He remembered that once into the tunnel it began to slope gently up. If they could reach higher ground . . .

It was like a huge white rose opening suddenly and dramatically as a torrent of water exploded from the cave mouth and dashed his hopes of salvation. The water hit the pair hard. Tom felt his legs go from under him. The lamp was torn from his hand and darkness filled the cavern.

Opposing currents tore at his body as five thundering torrents of water met and vied for supremacy. Emma was torn from his grasp as he was spun and turned in the currents. He was dashed against a boulder, the breath almost knocked from his body. At last he broke the surface of the water, coughing and spluttering, the intense darkness almost suffocating him.

He reached out blindly with his hands and felt hard, rough rock graze his palms. He hooked his fingers as he was dragged along in the pitch-darkness. His feet and knees hit objects below the water, the depth of which could not be more than chest-high, but the current prevented him from getting his feet down. At last the fingers of his right hand found a niche in the wall and he held onto the rough edge that presented itself. This enabled him to get his feet down and he managed to stand; the water level was just above waist-height.

He had no idea whereabouts he was in the cavern until a flash of lightning lit up the opening and gave him a brief glimpse of his surroundings.

He had been swept from one side of the cavern to the other and was now standing against the far side wall of the chamber, a few yards up from the tunnel mouth. Water was still flowing from it, but not with the same intensity.

He felt sick at heart at the thought of Lakota George and Emma, their bodies broken and twisted at the bottom of the chasm and a fierce anger broke through the grief. He vowed that Jake Bundy would pay dearly for the tragedy he had caused.

He listened to the thunder; the storm was moving away, the lightning getting less and less. He waited for each flash to give him a glimpse of different areas of the cavern. The back wall next to the three tunnels offered the best hope. Boulders were stacked there and it had been the place where Lakota George had found the wood for the fire.

He moved slowly towards the rear of the cavern on legs that were numb from the coldness of the water. Gratefully he hauled himself on to the boulders clear of the water and collapsed, exhausted.

12

Night had long since fallen. Bart Lorimer shuddered in his office as the lightning danced behind a curtained window followed by a crash of thunder. The front of the bank had been boarded up following the explosion that had blown the door and frame out and shattered the windows, but his office, at the back, had been untouched. Though the bank was closed until proper repairs could be made, he still had work to do.

He poured himself a generous measure of whiskey and tossed it down in a single gulp. The lamp on the desk, which surrounded him in a pool of light, lit up a sheen of sweat dappling his pudgy features. Things were going badly wrong and he was scared.

Bottle and glass rattled together as he poured himself another drink. The door opened, making him jump. He grabbed for the gun on the desk top, but relaxed as the figure moved to the edge of the pool of light.

'Oh, it's you; 'bout time too.' His teeth clinked on the edge of the glass as he swallowed half the whiskey this time. He wiped his lips with a trembling hand. 'I want my share. I'm getting out of here, away from Prospect before it's too late.' The figure did not move or make a reply. 'Do you hear me, dammit!' Lorimer's voice went up an octave. Lightning and thunder answered him. The former jigging a wild fandango in the window-frame as the latter roared out its delight. 'It's getting too dangerous here,' Lorimer went on. 'I . . . What are you doing man!' Lorimer's eyes popped. He came to his feet, the chair tipping over behind him. He made a grab for the gun, but a gun that had appeared in the other's hand spoke first.

In a crash of thunder the gun spoke twice and two bullets ripped into the banker's heart, smashing through ribs, driving splinters of bone deep into the wildly beating heart, tearing it to pieces.

Bart Lorimer was dead before he hit the floor. He never even heard the quiet closing of the door as the killer left.

★   ★   ★

He must have fallen asleep. Tom jerked awake and the cold, grey light of dawn filled the cavern. He groaned as he moved. His body was cold, joints stiff, flesh numb. He managed to sit up. The flood waters had ceased sometime during the night and only a few pools of water dotted about the cavern floor remained.

He slithered down from his rocky perch and went to his knees on the cavern floor, his legs refusing to support him. He groaned and cursed as the movement set his limbs afire with painful pins and needles as the circulation came back.

A sound caught his ears and he

stiffened, head snapping up. Water dripped, mingling with his own harsh breathing. There it was again. A sob, a groan and his heart began to beat faster. He climbed to his feet. His legs shook, but this time they supported him.

'Emma!' His call echoed back to him from the walls. He must be imagining things.

'Tom.' Weak and faint he heard his name called.

'Emma!' he called again, hardly daring to believe that she could still be alive. His own aches and pains forgotten he began moving around the cavern, eyes searching, heart beating fast.

'Over here, Tom.'

He found her hunched in a narrow cavity only yards from the opening into the chasm. Swept there by the water, she had managed to hold on. He helped her out and held her tight in his arms.

People had gathered outside the bank in Prospect, watching in silence as the body of Bart Lorimer was carried out and laid on the undertaker's handcart in the early morning sun.

'Dammit, Hoyt, who'd wanna kill the banker?' Mitch Colson pondered. 'First the mayor, now the banker.'

'We know who killed the mayor,' Nokes growled. 'Reckon the same person killed the banker.'

'Morgan came back here?' Colson looked puzzled. 'Why would he do that?'

'How in tarnation would I know?' Nokes grated irritably. 'He an' the banker had no love for each other, so mebbe Morgan decided to get rid of him.'

'What you gonna do, Sheriff?' The crowd had moved around the two as the undertaker pushed his cart away.

'Get you boys mounted and out looking. It's Tom Morgan for sure. This time we don't take no chances.' He raised his voice. 'Kill him an' anyone with him on sight.'

★　★　★

'What are we going to do, Tom?' Emma asked. The light in the cavern had grown stronger as the sun climbed higher in the sky outside. She had recovered from the night's ordeal and asked the question that Tom had no answer for, yet.

Tom moved fretfully around the cavern. He had found one saddle, washed into a corner, with a lariat still attached. He felt that the rope would come in useful, so it was now over his shoulder.

'Can't go back the way we came. Without light we'd get lost for sure. Some o' them caves we passed through had more'n one tunnel leading off. If'n we took the wrong one . . . ' He left the rest unsaid.

'Well, we can't stay here,' Emma

prodded worriedly.

'No, ma'am,' Tom agreed, his mind elsewhere as he peered into the three caves at the rear of the cavern.

'What are you thinking?'

'Reckon if'n the water can get in then mebbe we can get out.'

He entered each tunnel in turn before returning to the middle one of the three. He spent some time in that one before emerging and sitting down on a boulder.

'Well?' she demanded.

'Need to crawl on your belly a bit, but it comes out at the bottom of a shaft that goes straight up. You can see light, but not where it's coming from. Guess the shaft sorta bends and wiggles. Could get up there an' find it's too small to get through.' He shrugged and looked up at her.

'So what are we waiting for? There's only one way to find out.' She spoke with a confidence she did not feel.

Tom smiled. 'Yes, ma'am,' he said crisply.

Her confidence drained even further as, a little later, she stood with Tom at the bottom of the shaft. It was roughly circular and about three feet wide. It looked narrower further up.

'How do we get up there?' Her voice croaked a little as she spoke.

'Reckon I can get up there using feet an' back. Sorta wriggle my way up an' then haul you up on the rope.' Now it was Tom's turn for a show of confidence. He hoped that whatever gods were watching over him last night were still on duty today. They were without food and he knew that in a couple of days they would not have the strength to do this. It had to be now and successful.

Using feet and back, pushing against each other to provide support, he found it easier than he thought, but after a while the rough walls of the shaft wore holes through his vest and shirt and began to tear at his flesh, leaving bloody marks on the walls.

Sweat was dripping off him when he

reached a point some twenty feet up where the shaft joined a ledge that burrowed back a few feet before joining the shaft once again. He had a tricky manoeuvre to perform because his feet were facing the lip of the ledge and he needed to be sideways so that he could get an arm in. But eventually he managed it and lay there breathing hard for a few minutes.

The light was stronger here and he couldn't restrain a whoop of delight when he saw a circle of blue sky at the top of the shaft.

It was relatively easy to lower the rope and haul Emma up to the ledge. Then using the same process as before, he inched his way up the shaft. This time he scarcely noticed the pain from his lacerated back or the ache in his legs. Freedom was within a few yards and with it a revenge he dearly wanted to exact.

It took almost an hour from the cavern to reach the top of the shaft. Tom hauled Emma out and they stood on the edge of the world enjoying the feel of the sun on their skin and drinking in the cool, caressing breeze.

They stood on the edge of a high mountain lake surrounded by ragged rimrock that had been breached by a hole close to where they had climbed out. Tom was in no doubt that the hole was man-made. Beyond the lake in all directions peaks soared, but to the east, between the peaks, they caught a glimpse of the ochre, Texas plain, stretching away until it merged with the sky in a purplish mist.

Emma was shocked at the sight of Tom's raw and bleeding back and she cleaned it, as best she could, with cool lake water. After a rest they began the perilous descent of the mountain. It was a slow journey and by the time they reached the trail that led up to Eagle Pass, they had acquired a fair collection of scrapes, bruises and cuts between them.

The part of the trail they stumbled wearily and thankfully on to was below the Snakepit and from here on it was a dreary trudge in the dusty heat to reach the valley below. Before nightfall they found a place to hole up and review a bleak situation. They had no food or horses and were in a hostile world that wanted them dead. Hardly the stuff for a dreamless night's sleep.

*   *   *

The saloon was crowded and noisy so that at first no one heard the cries of the excited man. Hoyt Nokes, at the bar with Mitch Colson, turned, bleary-eyed. Someone was talking to him. It was Milt Dooley, one of the posse leaders.

'What you saying, Milt?' Nokes roared above the bedlam.

'We got 'em, Sheriff. Morgan an' the girl.' He turned and waved towards the batwings. A few seconds later Tom and Emma were ushered in, followed by a dozen or so other posse members.

A hush settled through the saloon as

the two were prodded forward to stand before Nokes.

A huge smile split Nokes's face.

'Well, well, now ain't that jus' dandy. Well done, Milt. Where'd you find 'em?'

'See'd 'em coming down the Eagle Pass trail. Walking, no horses, then followed 'em till they was ready to bed down for the night an' stepped right up an' arrested 'em,' Milt sang out proudly.

'Where's the Injun?'

'Dead, they said.'

Nokes eyed Tom's taut face.

'Is that a fact. Pure shame. Means we got only two to hang.'

'The girl has nothing to do with it. Let her go,' Tom said.

'After she set you free from a hanging. You an' this little hell-cat are gonna swing together. Why'd you kill the banker? Found poor ol' Bart shot dead in his office this morning.'

Tom stared at Nokes.

'I don't know what you mean,' he said weakly.

Nokes shrugged. 'Never no mind, you're gonna hang anyway.'

'Do you want someone to get Mace?' a voice called out.

'No, jus' a rope, two ropes.' Nokes looked up at the rafters overhead, his smile even wider as he returned his gaze to Tom and Emma. 'We'll do it here, now.'

'They'll be no hanging here or anywhere, Nokes.'

Heads craned around at the sound of the voice. Nokes looked between the two as Seth Haggerman and a half-dozen other men entered the saloon. They were carrying rifles.

Nokes stepped clear of the two and faced the sombre-faced Seth. His lip curled derisively as he eyed the group; they were the town's business community. Sober, churchgoing, God-fearing men.

'Well, well. D'you boys know how to use them guns? They might go off an' frighten you,' he jeered, raising a chuckle from those nearest.

'We served our time in the war, Nokes. Did our fair share o' killing an' was glad when the war was over to hang our guns up, but we never forgot how to use 'em. Never thought we'd need 'em again, but times have changed,' Seth Haggerman said.

'Sure have,' Nokes agreed. 'But afore you go waving them smoke-poles 'bout, look around. There's more'n forty guns in here.'

'If'n they are fool enough to die for you then so be it.' Seth Haggerman's face remained set. 'Listen up, you men.' He raised his voice as he pulled a square of paper from a vest pocket. 'I did what Nokes here should have done. I contacted Sheriff Lomax of Pine Ridge a coupla days ago an' he confirmed that Tom Morgan was with him when Mayor Tully was killed. Sheriff Lomax is on his way here to clean up this mess Nokes and Colson have made.'

A buzz of whispered conversation greeted his words.

'How'd we know that this Lomax ain't in cahoots wi' Morgan an' they cooked up this story 'tween 'em?' Nokes shouted out.

''Cause I ain't in the business o' lying, mister!' For a second time heads craned around and Sheriff Lomax, accompanied by three, dark-suited, gun-toting deputies entered. 'Bin hearing things 'bout this town, Nokes, an' when I got Mr Haggerman's wire, figured it was 'bout time I came an' took a look for myself.' He glowered around. 'Reckon I arrived just in time. Cut them loose.' He spoke to the nearest seated man, who hopped to do the big sheriff's bidding quickly.

'Now see here. I'm the law in Prospect,' Nokes began.

Lomax swung around on Nokes.

'Mister, you ain't fit to wear a badge. Now if'n you've a mind to argue with me, then we'll settle it right here and now.'

Nokes's face whitened and he took a step back, raising a hand before him.

'I ain't arguing, Sheriff,' he replied.

While Lomax and Nokes faced each other, Tom had moved to where Colson had thrown his gunbelt. Now, with the gunbelt settled about his waist and tied down at the thigh, Tom, grim-faced, stepped to Lomax's side.

'If'n you don' mind, Sheriff, Nokes an' me have got some long overdue settling to do. Him an' Colson killed the Blakes and set up Ethan Small for the killings.'

A shocked hush filled the saloon and all eyes focused on Nokes and Colson.

'Now is that a fact,' Lomax drawled, staring hard at the two.

'Got me the evidence,' Tom said evenly.

'You got nothin',' Nokes spat back, but a sheen of sweat glistened on his face. 'You're bluffin'.'

'Like I'm bluffing about my left-handed draw. You ready to find out, Nokes? Kill me and the evidence dies with me. How about it, Nokes, am I bluffing?' There was a mocking note in his voice.

'Tom, you can't,' Emma cried out. 'Sheriff Lomax, you can't allow this.'

'Good people have died. Now it's personal. It's time to settle up,' Tom said.

Sheriff Lomax eyed Tom's set profile.

'Let's say I haven't arrived yet. You boys keep an eye on that other ranny. If he moves, shoot him.'

'I ain't moving,' Colson yelled, hands flying into the air.

'Just you and me now, Nokes,' Tom prodded in the tense silence that had settled, thick and heavy in the saloon. 'Kill me and you walk away free; I called you out. Ain't that right, Sheriff?'

'Without any evidence, that's the truth o' it,' Lomax agreed. Hoyt Nokes licked his dry lips, his hand hovering over the butt of his pistol, eyes locked on Tom. He said nothing and his eyes gave nothing away as he went for his gun.

Nokes was fast, but the shot that rang out did not come from his gun. His gun had not levelled on his opponent when a bullet ripped into his right shoulder, shattering the joint before lodging against the shoulder-blade. The bullet spun him, the gun flying unfired from his grasp as he sprawled to the floor sending a table and three chairs crashing down. As he lay there, clutching his injured shoulder and groaning in agony, Tom appeared in his misty vision.

'You didn't think death would be that easy did you, Nokes? The hangman's waiting for you an' Colson.'

It was too much for Colson.

'It was Tully's idea. He wanted them dead an' Nokes here did the killing.'

There was uproar in the saloon, which Lomax quieted after a few minutes.

'Damned if'n you folk in Prospect don't know how to entertain a man.'

'Bear with me, Sheriff. There's just one more part of the puzzle to sort out.'

* * *

'I hear the banker got his'sel killed.'

In the gloom of the livery stable lit only by a single lamp hung from a beam, Jake Bundy jumped, startled by the sudden voice. He turned as Tom Morgan walked towards him.

'Tom. How'd you . . . ?'

'Get outta the Snakes? It wasn't easy. Lakota George died there. But then we were all supposed to, weren't we, Jake?' Tom came to a halt before Jake.

'I don't know what you mean,' Jake protested.

Tom smiled thinly.

'I reckon you knew that we were sitting under a lake and when it rained those caves filled with water. A stick o' dynamite sure helped the process along.'

'I ain't too sure what you're on 'bout, Tom?' There was an edginess to Jake's voice.

'That wheel hanging outside, over the doors — that came from the wagon the lost patrol were escorting that night. The wagon never left here, did it, Jake.

The men in the patrol were tired, relaxed 'cause they were in friendly hands. They didn't expect to be eating bullets for supper that night.'

Jake shook his head.

'You mus' be feverish, Tom. If'n you want a horse to get outta town . . . ?'

'You didn't kill Ethan Small because you thought he was going to kill me, you killed him because of what he might have told me. Blake was on to you. You told Tully and he had Nokes and Colson kill him. Colson confessed that much. You mebbe heard the shooting earlier. That was Nokes being persuaded that confession is good for the soul. Colson didn't need no persuasion.'

'You can't prove any o' what you're saying, boy,' Jake said coldly.

'I think I can.' Tom moved to the stall that Jake kept filled with hay bales. He heaved one out and bent down. 'The gold wagon never left Prospect and what better place is there to hide a wagon than in with a lot of other wagons, and the gold . . . ' He straightened up. In one hand he held a 'brick' from the floor of the stall. Its face-up side was painted grey, but the sides and bottom shone gold in the lamplight. 'Painted to look like stone. Covered with hay; no one would ever know. Very clever. What did you do? Just take a few bars at a time?'

'You're too clever for your own good, Tom Morgan,' Jake snarled. His hands were now filled with a shotgun which he held unwaveringly on the other. 'Now drop the gold.'

Tom shrugged, but did as he was asked.

'So humour me, Jake. How did your plan for the gold work?'

'Sure, why not. You ain't gonna be telling anyone,' Jake said ominously. 'The banker sold the gold for us. Trouble is he started to get scared when you started to poke about. Then, after Tully was killed he wanted out, to get away wi' what was left o' his share. Couldn't let that happen, so I paid him a visit on the way back from the Snakes.'

'So you killed him. Why did you kill Tully?'

'You made him panic. He was drawing attention to himself that coulda led back to us an' we couldn't let that happen.'

'Us?' Tom looked thoughtful. 'Let me figure this out. Tully an' Lorimer were on the town council an' so were Trimble, Clayton and Seth Haggerman, though I can't believe Seth was involved.'

Jake's face cracked in a smile.

'Seth wasn't. He just made the council look good. Genuine voice o' the townsfolk. You sure are smart, Tom, but not smart 'nough to dodge a bullet. Caught you sneaking 'bout trying to steal a horse an' shot you, that's how I'll tell my story.'

'How did you find out about Blake?' Tom pressed on.

'You were right 'bout the wheel. He recognized it an' then the damn fool went an' told Tully. He said there was a tintype of the wagon that would prove the wheel came from it an' he was going to Pine Ridge to get it.'

'So Tully sent Nokes and Colson to take care of the Blakes and lay the blame on Ethan Small.'

'Somebody had to take the blame,' Jake said casually.

'You picked up my knife at the river.'

'Meant to give it back, but then found another use for it.' Jake laughed. 'I like you, Tom, pure shame you gotta die.'

'Not this time, Jake.' Tom raised his voice. 'You can come in, Sheriff. I hope you heard everything?'

'Every word.' Sheriff Lomax entered followed by Seth Haggerman heading a bunch of townsfolk.

Jake looked around wildly and whirled as the three deputies entered at the other end.

'Ain't no way out, Jake. You killed innocent and guilty alike for your greed, now it's time to pay,' Tom said coldly.

'Damn you, Morgan!' Jake turned

and faced Tom, swinging the shotgun to cover him. His finger was whitening on the trigger when Tom drew his own gun with lightning speed and rattled off two shots. The bullets smashed into Jake's chest, shattering bone as they tore into his heart. Jake spun, already dead when the shotgun roared as his dead finger spasmed on the trigger, sending the shot harmlessly peppering the under-side of the hay-loft before Jake sank to his knees and toppled forward.

Tom reholstered the gun.

'Tom!' Emma burst through the men and flew to his side wrapping her arms around him.

'Yep. You sure do know how to entertain a man,' Sheriff Lomax applauded with a grin. 'They'll be a sizeable reward for the recovery of the gold. Mind, I reckon you've got your own piece o' gold there.' He winked at Tom. 'Ma'am.' He touched the brim of his hat and smiled as he turned away. 'Let's go an' arrest these other varmints.'

We do hope that you have enjoyed reading this large print book.

Did you know that all of our titles are available for purchase?

We publish a wide range of high quality large print books including:
Romances, Mysteries, Classics
General Fiction
Non Fiction and Westerns

Special interest titles available in large print are:
The Little Oxford Dictionary
Music Book, Song Book
Hymn Book, Service Book

Also available from us courtesy of Oxford University Press:
Young Readers' Dictionary
(large print edition)
Young Readers' Thesaurus
(large print edition)

For further information or a free brochure, please contact us at:
Ulverscroft Large Print Books Ltd.,
The Green, Bradgate Road, Anstey,
Leicester, LE7 7FU, England.
Tel: (00 44) **0116 236 4325**
Fax: (00 44) **0116 234 0205**

BADGE OF EVIL

Andrew Johnston

Lawyer Jack Langan left New York to travel out west to meet the father who had abandoned him. But he didn't expect to be offered the richest ranch in the territory — or imagine that he would be abducted. And he certainly could not have envisaged challenging the sheriff to a gunfight in front of an angry crowd of townspeople . . . For Langan to survive, he must discover his own courage and learn to understand the ways of the West.

BUZZARD'S BREED

David Bingley

When Jim Storme went to join his brother Red, and his cousin, Bart McGivern, in Wyoming, he was heading for trouble. Cattle barons were attacking lesser men, and branding them as rustlers ... Jim joined the cattlemen's mercenaries, but he changed sides when confronted by his brother, Red. When a wagon loaded with dynamite hit their ranch, it was one of many clashes between settlers and invaders in which the three Texans made their mark, and struggled to survive.

'LUCKY' MONTANA

Clayton Nash

Sean Rafferty wanted money to buy back the ruins of his family's estate in Ireland. He didn't care how he got that money or how many lives he ruined in the process . . . A man called 'Lucky' Montana found that fate threw him into the deal. With a bounty hunter already stalking him, Montana now had to contend with Rafferty's murderous crew as well . . . Now he must stride into battle, knowing that there is always a bullet waiting for him.

THE RYDER BRAND

Mike Stall

Jack Ryder had had enough of killing in the Civil War and, indeed, had barely survived. Now, working as an attorney, he'd come out West for a quiet life. However, Dutton Mazer, whose family own the biggest spread thereabouts, picks a fight with Jack. Then his father, Bull Mazer, tries to take over the entire range by resorting to kidnapping and arson . . . But when they stoop to murder, Jack must pin on a star and fight fire with fire, bullet with bullet . . .

DARROW'S BADGE

Gillian F. Taylor

Sapphires and diamonds: to Sir Hugh Keating, aristocrat and Govan town deputy, the jewellery is the dowry for his future wife. To Black Elliot and his gang, Keating's jewellery means prestige. When the gems are stolen, there's trouble for Sheriff Darrow. Black Elliot stays one jump ahead of the law, but fights to control his men. Darrow's right to wear his badge is threatened and, for both men, the battle of wits will finish in a cloud of gunsmoke.

VULTURE GOLD

Chuck Tyrell

Garet Havelock was Vulture City's marshal when outlaw Barnabas Donovan sent his men to rob $100,000 in bullion from the Vulture Mine headquarters. Chasing the thieves across the Mojave Desert, Jicarilla Apaches forced Havelock and Donovan's bunch together in a cave on Eagle Eye Mountain. Then there was Laura Donovan, the outlaw leader's half-sister . . . Now Havelock must survive the Apache 'run of death', and face Donovan's gunslingers to get the gold and the girl.